Shadowland

GJ Wielinga

Shadowland

Shadowland appeared for the first time in 2008 in
the Dutch language as 'Schaduwland'.

Copyright © 2023 GJ Wielinga

ISBN: 9789081428873

CONTENTS

PROLOGUE

Amsterdam, December 2023

Dear reader,

When was the last time you were in love? Do you still remember how it felt?

This novella was written in 2006 and is a fair representation of my life at that time. Although, as a child, I filled entire notebooks with self-made stories, the writing bug truly hit me later, around 2001. At the time, I was deeply interested in advertising agencies and thought it wise to pursue a distance-learning course in copywriting. The first lesson was an introduction: 'tell something about yourself.' Back then, everything was still done on paper through mail. I distinctly remember the feeling when I read the note in the margin from the attending teacher. 'Finally, someone who can write!' I really didn't need any further encouragement.

The copywriting course officially lasted two years, but four months later, I held my certificate and realized I had higher ambitions than just crafting creative marketing texts. I wanted literary. A period followed with numerous visits to the library. Three days a week, I worked in a dirty gay bar in the center of Amsterdam; the rest of the time, I was reading and experimenting with short stories. Books that left a lasting impression on me were Georges Perec's 'Un homme qui dort', Gustave Flaubert's 'Madame Bovary', Friedrich Nietzsche's 'Ecce Homo', and my ultimate reading pleasure was Johann Wolfgang von Goethe's 'Die Leiden des jungen Werthers'.

Back to 2006. I turned 35 that year and was now working for a communication agency. The previous year had been a dizzying flight of bold moves. I quit the dirty gay bar because I disagreed with the new owners. My attempts to rally the rest of the staff against them had failed. In London, my New Zealand ex stole the small fortune I had set aside to start a new life there. Back in Amsterdam, I started working in another gay bar where the alcoholic regulars made my life miserable. The Italian dancer with whom I maintained a fuck buddy relationship turned out to be terrified of HIV, and after asking my South African roommate to rent a room somewhere else, I realized, alone, that I was too depressed to handle bar work. My Swiss ex, fresh out of a relationship with two muscle Marys from Milan, wanted me to come paint his apartment in Zurich. Back in Amsterdam, after a humiliating visit to the employment agency, I thankfully found a job at the communication agency of Fred and Eric. I was hired as a secretary but turned out to be a quick-learning assistant. That's how I rolled into 2006, and that's where this story begins.

The story consists of three parts. In the first part, you see me living life to the fullest, falling in love, and hitting a wall. Part two covers the day when, due to stress, half of my face becomes paralyzed, and I reflect on death. In part three, I try unsuccessfully to find myself again.

In this version, I replaced the pseudonyms from the first Dutch edition with the real names. It's been so long now that it probably doesn't matter anymore. Besides, I don't write truly negative things about the people who crossed my path at that time. The only one who comes off poorly is myself. According to the reviewer from gay magazine Winq, I sound 'just like a bitch.' My debut received the comment 'maniacal' in an online store. In a book reading club, someone marveled at how easily she could identify with a man falling in love with another man, and the reviewer from the literary gay archive IHLIA thought it was a shame that a novella that opened so brilliantly faded like a candle in the night. Another person found the novella stylish and daring in terms of style and structure but found the protagonist very unsympathetic. And a reviewer who also wrote books about male love couldn't resist tearing the work apart with much delight, his pen dripping in jealous ink.

Meanwhile, I had a falling out with my publisher, a chain-smoking thirty-something who lived with his parents in Valkenburg, in the most southern corner of the Netherlands. There had been interest from the Herengracht in Amsterdam, where all the prominent Dutch publishers were located at that time. A short absurd story in a literary magazine had brought them on my track. But when I presented 'Schaduwland', it was difficult. Homoeroticism didn't sell, they said. Valkenburg seemed not to mind homoeroticism, and with a bit of imagination, I saw in him a brilliant young publisher with whom I would storm the literary world. Unfortunately, he turned out to be an amateurish bungler.

First, there was an editor who poured my tightly structured staccato sentences into flowing round shapes. A bad start. I stood my ground. Alongside Valkenburg, I did the editing work because the budget was exhausted. There was also no budget for design. Good friends Marc and Vincent offered to take care of that. Now Valkenburg stood his ground. Battered and full of typos, the work emerged from the printer after six months of waiting. By then, I had already postponed the launch once. Eventually, I also handled all the publicity myself.

The bizarre thing is that as a novice writer, you want someone to publish you. Of course, to handle the entire printing process, distribution, and publicity. But more than that, for the recognition. Finally, you can call yourself 'author.' But I also understood from the publishers on the Herengracht and from writers published there that selling books is quite a complex endeavor. A writer with a very sensitive pen who also wrote a lot about male love told me that his publisher didn't earn anything from his books, but they included him in their fund because they needed a gay writer in order to take themselves seriously. His books were funded by the proceeds from the books of a popular sports commentator.

Years later, my Valkenburg-based publisher was declared bankrupt. Should I buy my books or should they go to the shredding machine? I chose the latter because I still disagreed with that first edition. I also realized that the rights to 'Schaduwland' had come back entirely into my hands. A few years later, I found out that someone had 'rescued' my stack of unsold books from the shredder and offered them for sale on the internet.

What can you do? Sue someone for theft and then, after much hassle and stress, make a few paltry euros? I'm doing it this way: self-publishing. Not ideal in terms of sales technique. Literary readers like to see the name of a prominent publisher, but perhaps this work should be read by a slightly less conventional elite.

As I write this, more than fifteen years have passed since the publication date of the first edition. It's almost eighteen years since I started writing this story. Of course, I noticed small things in the text that needed to be adjusted. The editing process was a mess back then. But all in all, I still stand fully behind this work, my debut. This is who I was and what I could do. The first time I spoke up. A small monument on the edge of madness.

After this impossible love story, I had one more major impossible love: an Australian with commitment issues. I traveled to Perth twice to find out that while love is grand and invincible, if one of the lovers is afraid of love, the cold reality is that love remains a beautiful illusion, driven by dopamine.

Even the relationship therapist who wanted me to love myself again, the astrologer who saw that a soulmate brought nothing but misery, and the reincarnation therapist who took me back to 1555 in the French Provence couldn't offer me more than a completely sober view of a far too romantic worldview.

And this is how I live nowadays. I was in love once more. With a Canadian living in Brooklyn. During corona. He did something with art and HIV, and I got to interview him via zoom. He flirted with me from the local beach, and I didn't exactly know why. But unconsciously, I had already shipped my furniture and my two cats to New York. After the interview, I went for a walk, and then, in utmost concentration and speed, I typed the piece and sent it to the magazine where it was supposed to appear. Then I spent two weeks weaning off the dopamine and bringing it back into its natural balance.

So, consider this novella as an ode to all those people who dream of love but, one way or another, can't attain it.

I SURVIVAL

You address me. Drunk. Me too. Drunk. Vodka. Delicious you. Beer. I estimate. What we're talking about, I no longer know. Are we talking? Something general. Something silly. Something unimportant. I follow you to the toilet. You follow me to the toilet. A kiss above the urinals. More kisses in the cubicle. T-shirts off. Belts undone. On your knees. Loud knocking from a guy who can't pee if someone's watching or needs to shit. Music stops. We have to leave. We want to stay. Party over. Lights on. Brooms on the dance floor. We go to my house. Or to yours. Around the corner. As you say. Your friend is waiting for you. You have a friend. He's waiting for you. You're messing around with me. I want a man like you. Cold. Sex. Playground for kids. Iron sphere of steel rods. Freezing. I want to snuggle up to you. Kiss you. Feel you. Smell you. Keep you with me forever. Come with me. It's late already. You say. Can I remember a number. I don't remember numbers.

Except yours.

Damn it.

Monday, January 2

NEVER DO THAT AGAIN

Tiger!

With sirens blaring at seven o'clock on New Year's morning in Madrid? Yelling on a stretcher? Losing control? Everything in chaos? I'm glad you're still alive. What luck you had someone with you. Imagine being somewhere else, completely lost, ending up comatose in a hospital. Respect. And what you said about needing to let out all the anger and frustration, that this was the moment to unload everything. Good for you. God knows the edges you've crawled along this past year. How everything exploded in your face, and yet you keep going. Those impossible jabs in your heart that numb you, startle you, and show you all the corners of the room.

By the way, do the colors I so vigorously smeared on your wall still suit you? Those two weeks with you were like balm. Of course, and you felt it too, a lot surfaced for me. It was funny that you told me almost all your friends label me as 'the boyfriend who suited you best.' It was a good time. And yes, we fit together very well. Although I was often a brat. Especially then. I'm glad you survived New Year's. NEVER DO THAT AGAIN.

My New Year's Eve was drunk and lustful. Vincent and Marc invited me along with some other friends. One of those friends, Shahryar, turned out to be interested in me. A hottie. Iranian, as far as I understood, but raised in Geneva. He's now in Paris, and I was quite disappointed that, after his initial advances, he didn't accept my invitation to come to my place for a bit more fun. The next morning, he was already on the train again. But I tracked down his email address. My first, cautious email was received enthusiastically.

Shahryar creates video art, and some of his work is displayed in the Appel. I plan to check it out sometime next week.

I've updated my profile again. To what I think I'm looking for. Not too revealing and very approachable. I must say, I have to contort myself into even stranger positions to get a good picture of myself. Those wrinkles are getting deeper. Perhaps the reason why, while I still can, I'm marketing myself so extensively. Another reason might be that by being busy with hunting, I think less about the things I really should be dealing with, like making money and finally publishing. This year, I promise you. I've written a lot in the past months. There's nothing yet that I want you to read. But it's in progress. Don't think I'm idling.

Christmas was absurd. The plan was to go to Spellbound with Vincent. I was ready in a black outfit and had smoked a fat joint when he called back. His father had just passed away. You don't expect that when you're going out for the evening. Too intense. So, I spent about half an hour on the phone with him. A strange conversation. Me stoned, and he just recovering from the initial shock. I even considered not going partying but, braving the cold, cycled to the back of the Vondelpark. Many memories surfaced from when my own father died. It's still a kind of impossible situation; death.

After a few vodkas, I felt a bit more cheerful, and I met a funny guy. When the lights came on, we were fooling around in the restroom. His name is Maurice, and he's completely my type. A lively, bouncy guy, very quick-witted, and it was so much fun in the restrooms that we wanted to continue our session somewhere else. Unfortunately, that wasn't possible. Outside, he told me his friend was waiting for him at home. We messed around a bit on the playground with our drunken heads, and if it hadn't been so cold, we probably would have succeeded in bringing it to a happy conclusion. Now I was cycling back home with a phone number in my head because I didn't have my mobile with me.

What are your plans now? Are you going to take it easy this week? So, I turn thirty-five on

Wednesday. I've taken the day off from work. I don't know yet what I'm going to do, but I'll definitely be home between six and eight. I kiss and hear from you!

Love from the old Wolf.

Friday, February 10

You mean that highwayman?

Yes, he's great, but the violated woman is also acting her heart out. Thank goodness for Kurosawa. Thanks for the recommendation!

Old Tiger,

Impressive, that travel schedule! Fortunately, all within Europe. Then you don't have to spend too many hours in the air. My friend Ymke has to go to Hong Kong all the time and developed a serious sleep problem last year. I'm glad you're doing better. You don't want such a severe flu too often. Are you taking your vitamins and everything?

Here, all is going smoothly. Work is fine. Nine to five is already becoming routine. It's bizarre, actually, that I've never done this before. No complaints about me. They are very easy-going with me. Yesterday, for example, I had to prepare about ten letters. It's unimaginable how many things can go wrong with that. I had to redo it five times, and even then, there were things that didn't add up. Do you write Mrs. Doctor Professor or Professor Doctor Mrs.? With or without capital letters? Abbreviated or in full? Precision. Inexperience. 'The devil is in the details,' as Eric said. He had to learn it himself at some point and takes plenty of time to explain it to me. I'm learning a lot. At least a sense of diligence.

My contact with Shahryar is somewhat less meticulous. I went to see his work at the Appel. Some big names there. Even a Nauman. You remember that retrospective at Kunsthaus? Madness. The work at the Appel wasn't terribly interesting. The theme was gravity. Lots of falling, rolling, shaking things.

Shahryar had his work in a side room. I had to cross the exhibition spaces three times before I found it. A reasonably interesting work in itself. A video of a failed suicide attempt on the Eiffel Tower. A bald man in a red T-shirt who ultimately decides not to jump. I wrote Shahryar an email about how okay this exhibition is. Since then, he treats me like a fan. I must say, it was also a disappointment that he turned out to already have a boyfriend with whom he lives. I found out in the third week. Suddenly, he no longer wrote 'I' but 'we.' Strange if you ask me. I felt like an intruder. All very unpleasant.

Meanwhile, I've started dating. I have to do something! I go on about three dates per week. More is undoable. I still remember having two sex dates a day easily during my manic periods, but that always backfired afterward. Mixing up faces and names, Not knowing if I had done it with someone or not, disappointed faces when *they found out I was swiftly moving from bed to bed. Painful.*

By the way, I'm going to Rome next month. Visiting Marc at the Swiss Institute. He had invited me so many times now that I couldn't refuse. I'm really looking forward to hanging out in that city. The last time was fantastic. Have I told you? Twenty. In love. His name was Filippo Morelli. Actor. On the back of his scooter. I googled him and found a pasta commercial where he plays the handsome daddy. There's also a Spanish movie with him as the 'man on the train.' It seems he's on screen for no more than a minute, but he still looks very hot. Quite a drama back then. Every time I called him, he cried. I thought because he missed me. Three guilders per minute. Expensive tears.

What are your plans now? Are you coming or not? Is it difficult to plan with all those conferences? Rembrandt-Caravaggio is on until somewhere in June. I saw on the news that the freezing cold from Russia is spreading across the continent. Get that thermal underwear out of the closet! Fortunately, you're first in Cannes for a few days. Lucky you.

LOVE from the old Wolf.

Somewhere between heaven and earth, angels float like wild cupids in search of victims. From their cloud, they aim their arrows especially at those who need it. You and I. We need it to break free from our own concentrated selves. To shockingly discover what our lives are worth and realize there is more. More than this. More than hunting around recklessly. More than impressing, dropping your pants for anything that even slightly smells like sex. Or lust. Or satisfaction. I don't know. I do know.

When I went to Rome and had an hour to wait, I was busy cruising by the toilets. They were downstairs at the gate. This way, I could precisely follow who wanted what when. I went downstairs a few times only to catch furtive glances, unfortunately. Oh well. It was only the first day of my vacation, so what did it matter?

It happened on the plane. I thought. A guy who had been sort of flirting with me while waiting sat two rows in front of me. He let his hand fall open while swinging his arm in the aisle. I was endlessly fascinated. He had black spiky neck hair and amusingly round ears. When he got up to go to the toilet, behind me on the plane, I gathered all my courage to follow him and see what would happen. Two flight attendants in their sky-blue uniforms, apron on, were filling trolleys. The cute guy closed the toilet door in my face. I nonchalantly waited to immediately sniff his scent when he was done. It smelled antiseptic. A kind of chlorine scent with a fragrance. Pine forest, sunny hill or vanilla. Unfortunately, I spent the whole flight with a limp.

In Rome, the first night felt like a shooting gallery. Many nice, tasty men. Marc took me on a pub crawl that ended at Circoli degli Artisti, where the guy was standing who had sent me videos of himself in the weeks before. Made with his phone. First jerking off and later fucking. Very unsafe fucking. He asked me if I liked barebacking, and I had to admit that, as a feeling, it felt physically pleasant, if not liberating. Psychologically, I always had a bit more trouble with it. So that man, let's call him Stefano, because that was his name, saw me and looked cheerful. I knew he wanted to have me and stayed close. I always enjoy being prey. You probably know the feeling: lure, probe, if he's a real man, he takes charge. Stefano came up to me, grabbed me with his rough hands forcefully at my hips, and pressed my backside into his crotch where I 'could experience his excited state in proximity.' He whispered with an incredibly hoarse voice in the kind of broken English that makes Italians so sexy. He was already taken that night, but if I wanted, he would dump that guy and fuck me in the ass in a way that I wouldn't want anything else anymore. I looked at Marc and decided to leave this bareback Italian for what he was. The guy he was going to fuck, by the way, was a real sissy.

A sort of show ballet dancer with big round tits
and a very high, round ass. Sometimes, just
taste is a problem.

Wednesday, March 15

RRRRRRRRRRRRRomAAAAAAAAAAAAAAA

Tigerrrrr,

Rome was fantastic! It went by way too fast. Before I left, I had already read some travel books and decided that the highlight of the trip would be ancient Rome. Standing in the middle of the Via Sacra is incredible, especially when you realize that this place was the center of the world two thousand years ago. It's like strolling around Manhattan today.

Marc picked me up on his motorino. It's just a short ride from Termini station to the institute, a beautiful old villa with some palm trees around it. The baroness who first ruled it hangs on a life-size canvas in the reception hall. I estimate her clothing from somewhere in the mid-nineteenth century. As you can imagine, everything is organized with Swiss precision. I felt right at home. The residents, including Marc, all have rooms on the fourth floor. From there, you already have a fantastic view of the city. But I found out that when you're in the little tower, where a studio is set up for an artist duo, you have a 360-degree view of the city around you. It's truly spectacular.

In the kitchen, on the same floor as the bedrooms, we would always find the other residents. I gave one of them, Frank from a small Swiss mountain village, some naughty dreams when I asked him to lock his room that night, or I would end up in bed with him. He was shocked and offended; he had never had to lock his door for such a reason, but at the same time, he made it clear that he appreciated my advances. I openly flirted with him, even though he showed me several times the photo of his extremely handsome boyfriend. That boyfriend was in Barcelona and turned out to be Shahryar's previous boyfriend.. Jawohl! Needless to say, quite an incestuous world those country men of yours. Some of Marc's drawings focus exactly on that.

I spent a lot of time in dark spaces during my stay in the Eternal City. The weather wasn't the best, rainy and cold. Several times, I felt like I would have a serious accident when I was riding on the back of Marc's motorino, racing through the rain over the cobblestones.

One night, eager to know how an ordinary Roman lives, I went with a guy who was very tall, lanky, and also very sweet. Giuseppe. We had coffee in a café behind Termini that was open all night, and then we took the bus to a suburb. He lived with a friend who had a spare room after her mother's death.

Because he wanted to tidy up his room first —'It's a mess,' he assured me—I spent the first fifteen minutes in a room that reminded me of *the interior of my mother's house, but in the Italian version. His room, despite his quick cleaning, was still a mess. But the bed was free, and that's what mattered in the end. The next day we talked a lot. Giuseppe was driven out of his village by his family because he likes men. He had something militant about him.*

Later that week, Marc introduced me to Luca. Super polished. Everything neat. The right shirt, the right pants, tidy shoes, well-cut hair. Always up for a good conversation, charming, well-mannered. I also went home with him. There, we smoked a joint, and then the beast was unleashed. He only wanted to have sex, and he did it several times. I felt completely disoriented. We didn't miss any positions. The couch, the table, the floor, and the wall all had their turn. The next day, I had several bruises in the most illogical places. But you can't say no to such a brutal natural force. Not much surprises me anymore, as you know, but I cannot deny that I was slightly amazed that the next morning there was no trace of the beast anywhere. As soon as we got out of bed, he changed the sheets, and an electrician who was installing his fast internet connection was led through the house with decisive courtesy. I was quite relieved to be back at the institute. It was only a five-minute metro ride.

The day before Luca, I was in the sauna. Marc felt unwell, and I was very curious about what happens in authentic Roman baths. Well, I can't recommend it unless you have an interest in mycology. There, without exaggeration, dozens of types of fungi grow in the most lush, smooth, and hairy varieties. Mostly dark green or brown, but I also saw light purple specimens. When I entered, I was given a shabby 'guide,' a narrow boy with drooping shoulders and greasy black slick hair, who would show me around the sauna. The first stop was a pitch-dark steam room that sharply smelled of urine. I felt how my 'guide' wanted to touch me, and it was quite tricky to find the door out. The walls were round and covered with moss (or so I told myself). I managed to leave the shabby guide in the room and when I saw him again, bewildered, with a questioning look in his eyes, I burst out laughing at him.

My first sexual encounter was in the smoking room above. Smoking is no longer allowed in public places in Rome, but you can always find a room with a kind of air conditioning that serves as ventilation. So here too. For convenience, there was a TV with a typical Italian quiz on it, and a few white plastic garden chairs were scattered around. A guy started giving me a blowjob. He had his eyebrows done, a rather bizarre trend to which many men in Rome seem to adhere. But otherwise, he was very nice and sucked well. Later, we went into a cabin, and I expertly screwed him on the fake leather-covered mattress. Together, we smoked a cigarette, and then I went in search of the next one. I was briefly in a cabin with a guy who not only felt quite ADHD but also came within a minute. There wasn't much fun to it. Even a possible conversation struggled to get started. He spoke good English, that wasn't the problem, but his conversation didn't go beyond listing all the major cities in Europe where he had been and what drugs he had used there. It didn't occur to him to ask me a question.

Feeling a bit unsatisfied, I hung out in one of the loungers set up in the corridor vault. After lying there a bit restlessly bored, I wanted to know what time it was. Marc had organized a dinner in the city, along with Frank and Luca, and we had agreed that I would be back at the villa by eight o'clock. It was already half past seven. But with the villa within walking distance, I decided to go back into the hot tub once more.

The architect of the hot tub had forgotten to build stairs. Otherwise, it was a spectacle; a rarely shaped concrete sculpture that was supposed to represent a rock formation but lacked imagination in crucial places. So it was climbing. Or jumping in from the higher part where the showers were constantly spraying. I lay like an effervescent tablet in a corner, and the poorly finished concrete scratched my back. I couldn't keep this up for long. I decided to take a shower. While I was trying to hoist myself out of the water, I gazed upon the most beautiful *physique I had seen in ages. The gorgeous body looked down, and the moment he stepped into the hot tub, I slipped. Startled, he fell, clumsily, onto me. We both burst into laughter, breaking the ice.*

From the conversation that ensued, I learned the handsome guy was named David, and he was on his way from Florence to Sicily, where his grandmother was on her deathbed. However, due to train schedules not aligning and a slight cold coming on, he had decided to visit this humid cellar. All of this was in Italian, which I didn't understand, although I caught on to a lot. It was immediately clear that all we wanted was to have sex with each other. But because I had to leave, it wasn't happening. Instead, we smoked a cigarette in the smoking room and passionately kissed. He wrote his phone number and email address on my T-shirt. It figures, meeting the most delicious person at a time when it's inconvenient. I even considered skipping dinner, but I realized Marc had organized it especially for me, and it would be an affront if I didn't show up. I was ten minutes late.

On my last evening in Rome, Marc took me to an exhibition by a Swiss artist. Following that, we had dinner at the home of a Roman family that collects art. The exhibition was a precisely crafted show with drawings of subtle lines on A4 sheets. In a corner, behind a wall, in a domed space, some plastic tableware was set up with a few spotlights on it, so the crooked shadows formed a finely designed shape on the rounded wall. Discussing the delicate lines and visual language of the artist, we headed to the family's house for the dinner. After the butler took our coats, we stood somewhat awkwardly at a table covered in white damask. After the second wine, everyone loosened up a bit. A lively conversation ensued between the curator, who was friends with Marc, a chubby guy dressed in lycra, and a tall man in a gray wool suit introduced to me as a retired curator and art critic. The latter couldn't take his eyes off me. The evening went smoothly, and Marc praised my presence with the words: "It's important to have people like you at these kinds of parties. Then everyone has something pleasant to look at."

Well. Oh yes, almost forgot. I went to see some Caravaggios to get an impression of what awaits us in Amsterdam. They have a beautiful one hanging in the Capitoline Museums. I had to wander through centuries of European paintings, but when I saw the canvas, I was completely overwhelmed. Caravaggio painted a painfully beautiful boy, sitting on a rock, with legs spread in a twisted posture. In the background, a ram's head emerges from the darkness. The other Caravaggios were in churches, and after inserting a coin, the light would come on for a minute. Is this how the church makes its income nowadays? I've never understood God. What I can't imagine is Rembrandt holding up well next to this daredevil. Everything is smooth and almost Hollywood. Dutch clumsiness, even if painted with the utmost sensitivity, is still no comparison, right? We'll see. I'm looking forward to your visit in May. Cool Tristan is coming along.

Baci, il Lupo vecchio.

Saturday, I ask: What?
You answer: Unk
I say: Yes

I no longer remember what expectations I had when I went to the Unk. I knew I would see you, but I didn't know what the effect would be. For the past three months, I've been drifting endlessly with the idea that if I were to encounter the right one, I would just know. Filling the meantime with bread and circuses. Dispelling boredom. Keeping busy. Not letting myself be defeated by feelings of discomfort. Making sure I stayed visible so that we would recognize each other when the time was there.

It can freeze. It can thaw. Sometimes Unk is full and super atmospheric, sometimes empty and desolate. Undoubtedly, the weather gods play a role in this decision. The evening we met, it was pouring rain. I was way too early. An empty dance floor. A video screen with a cult classic. A bar with bored staff. Music that doesn't know where to go. Groups of people hanging around, anticipating, realizing that nothing is happening here. Light seeking empty space.

As soon as we see each other— Do we know who the other is?—we can't believe what we see. You're so much more delicious than I can remember. Is it you? I want to devour you. You're devourable. Kiss you. Can I kiss you? Smell you. You smell amazing. Touch you. Instinct. I see you startle. You want it too. Let me in. Unrestrained. We lie down on a bench and make out. It's ridiculous. It's amazing. We go. To my place. Cycling in the rain. It's a mess at my home. Didn't expect you to be in my bed. Didn't expect this to be allowed. You're so beautiful. It makes me shy. You kiss me wherever I want. I hold you tighter. Go. Let go. Tomorrow doesn't exist. No yesterday. No right now. Everything is now. Here. In our arms. We hold each other as if we'll never let go. We laugh. Look at each other. Perfect. Not hard. Not harder. Detached from ourselves. Together. Do we realize that there's no stopping now? Do we know that the floodgates are open? That, even with the best will in the world, we'll never let go of each other ever again? That this is our eternity? No turning back. Never again.

I am slowly rocking in my hammock and can only smile. Dream. Stare at the ceiling. Float. On clouds. Slowly drifting away on that pink cloud. Until the moment I realize that you're not here and can't be here because you have another life. I can fall in love with you, but what's the use? I would only hurt myself. People in a relationship choose the relationship nine out of ten times, and the other is left with empty hands and a black heart. In this case, that other would be me.

Get up. Now. Put on pants. Now. Put on a sweater. Now. Put on your shoes. Now. But I don't want to. You have to. Put on your coat. Don't forget your condoms. And your keys. I don't want to. You have to. Walk to that bar. Now. Doesn't matter. You have no choice. You're

not allowed to fall in love. Under no
circumstances. Go inside. Order a vodka. Now.
Walk upstairs. Wait until a booth is free. Stand in
the booth, hang your sweater on the hook, and
wait for a dick to come out of the wall. Now.
Suck this cock. Is it firm enough? The right size?
If it feels good in your mouth, it's the right size
for your ass. Grab your condom. Don't whine.
Come on! Tear open the packaging while you
suck. It's a good dick, and it will snap you out of
your stupor. I promise you. Roll the condom over
the dick. Very good. Is it okay? Where's the
lube? In your pocket? What are you waiting for?
Take it out. Throw a good blob on the cock
that's ready. Turn around. Lower your pants.
Slide your ass against the cock. Make sure it
goes in all at once. It hurts less that way. Hold
onto the wall in front of you. Start fucking.
Come on! Fuck that cock. Let the booth go back
and forth. Let it creak and crack. Shout if you
have to. Come. Don't puke now. Wait until the
other is out of the booth or make sure you're
gone before he comes out. Don't listen to that
voice from the hole saying it was delightful. You
decide that. You have to go. Home. Sleep.
You've done the job. Are you still in love? No?
Good. Keep at it.

Monday, March 27

Feierabend galore!

Dearest Tiger,

I'm busy! You wouldn't believe it. I started writing a newsletter and now I'm working on two pieces. A story about online dating, which made it through the editorial process without too much damage, and a piece about glory holes. You can imagine that the research goes beyond just interviews. In the past two weeks, I've spent more time on my knees than an average monk. And the writing is enjoyable too.

On the dating front, things have been booming since I updated my profile. I realized I came across as a bit old-fashioned. That has changed now. I took some photos of myself that are both revealing and mysterious, and I still look relaxed! The latter was actually a prerequisite. Since then, no shortage of handsome guys. The tastiest one is Jason. An American with amazing eyes and a very naughty nose. I can't describe it any other way. We talk a lot when we're together. He calls himself 'cool and relaxed.' Believe me, it's the right description. When I screw him, he comes hands-free, and he is flattered when I beg him to stay the night. Then he never does because he has a dog to walk. But the pleasantness of his personality struck me. He gives yoga classes for 35 euros per hour and is taking the integration course. Learning Dutch in six months. I promised him some books to read, although he is a bit skeptical about the Netherlands. It's not strange: I am part of a particularly blunt people. Foreigners, with due courtesy, call it direct. Never tell a farmer he's a farmer.

Also, the Maurice story suddenly came to life. I don't know if I told you about him, but I met him somewhere in December. A married man, yes, but nowhere in his behavior does that seem to be a problem. When I was in Rome, the contact suddenly revived, probably because I brought my phone with me. We met last Saturday at the Unk. Because it was really boring, and we were too horny, we went to my house. I was still working on that internet story that I had printed out, and he unabashedly started reading it. He immediately bragged about his own writing, saying that people say he has a good sense of language. He told me about the stage performances he wrote, directed, and acted in. I felt like I had Molière visiting, and became a bit timid. Such a nice guy doing everything I ever aspired to. It's not like he can make a living out of it. He confessed that he works four days a week in a hospital as a theater therapist. I can imagine all sorts of things about what that entails, and the sex was good too. That was the ultimate goal. At quarter past five, he cycled away to, I assume, meet his friend at half past six. The next day, I hung dreamily in my hammock. I like this man more than all the others. But, as I said, not a good plan because he's already in a relationship.

I understand that you've been through a bit of a wild time? Tristan sounds like a very nice, sweet, and sensible guy. Quite a hassle that he just moved to Lausanne. How many hours is that by train? A nice journey, right through the country. And, if you ask me, Lake Geneva is one of the most beautiful places in the world. When the train comes out of the tunnel, and you have this wide view over the lake with the mountains behind it... I envy you!

David, the guy I met in the sauna in Rome, is coming in two weeks. I want to take him to Rembrandt-Caravaggio. I'll give you a detailed report.

See you soon, and kisses from your old Wolf

So, you have every Friday off, you triumphantly declared. So, we could meet every Friday. So, we could regularly have sex. Sex is healthy. It relaxes the muscles and releases chemicals in your brain that make you happy. So, I'm addicted to chemicals that make you happy.

Saturday, April 15

Endive mash with bacon

Dear Tiger,

Everything is fine here. David arrived after a somewhat strange exchange of letters. I'm not exactly sure what he's after, but at the moment, he's lying stoned in my hammock. It's the same guy I met in Rome. It was a bit exciting when he arrived. You're not sure what the expectations are. We were already fooling around on the first night. He has a kind of passive-aggressive demeanor and likes to be taken. I have no issues with that, and he's quite tasty. I did let him know immediately upon his arrival that I'm in love with someone else. Since we communicate with hands and feet, it was complicated. I showed him a photo of Maurice and tried to explain the situation. David didn't understand a thing, especially what the reason would be for me to bother him with my feelings for someone else. I can understand that, but I wanted to say it before it got complicated.

Caravaggio is amazing. There are a total of fourteen of his works, and except for a few paintings that have been copied so much they now seem kitsch, each one is overwhelming. You'll see it with your own eyes. The curator of this exhibition deserves a statue. It's so incredibly contemporary. A big bank sponsors it all. All the paintings are tastefully displayed across three halls, and since they had to find a connection with the Rembrandt year, there are also fourteen paintings by that master. Sort of thematic, as you often find in children's books. Initially, I thought I would have to visit this exhibition twice. First for the Rembrandts and then for the Caravaggios, but now that I've walked through it, I can't imagine wanting to see Rembrandt again near that overwhelming Italian painting style. Judge for yourself. It's literally and figuratively a challenge, this show.

David thought it was all nice. I don't think he easily gets grabbed by brushstrokes. He'd rather smoke and get laid. I don't know exactly what I owe all this to. In love with a ridiculously delicious, albeit unreachable guy and a perfect ass next to me in bed. Maurice also got in touch. It was clear that he wasn't comfortable with me having visitors. I like that, a bit of jealousy. It turns me on.

Last Friday, we had plans. He—Maurice—has Fridays off, just like me, and suggested making it a habit to see each other on that day. We agreed to meet at eleven, but he was there at twenty to eleven. He didn't dare to look at me at first, which I found sweet. He smelled like shaving soap. He's bald and shaves the rest of his head, except for his eyebrows, which run from one ear to the other. He has superb eyes and a nose that, as he noted himself, the tip of *which moves a bit with his mouth when he laughs. He has an insanely beautiful laugh with perfectly white teeth. When I told him that I had walked on clouds all day last Sunday, progress was made. He admitted that he had also lost his way a bit. We didn't do much. Mostly lying naked in the hammock, kissing, and a bit of sex. As if we were stoned.*

We went to lunch at Small World, and then it was easier to talk. About theater and acting. He has formed a theater group around him. According to him, 'a bunch of misfits,' and last year they had a show that they toured to many festivals. I'm very curious about his work. Afterward, we went back home and spent another couple of hours fooling around naked in the hammock. It's really too cozy with this guy. When he had to leave, I was genuinely sad that he couldn't stay and that I can't see him more often. I spent the whole evening staring at the ceiling.

But well. Things are as they are. He has his life, and I basically have one too.

David is starting to wake up. I'm going to stop. I bought ingredients for endive mash, just the way you like it. Talk to you later.

Love from the old Wolf

Twenty minutes. You are too early. Your head freshly shaved. You are a man who conceals his baldness by shaving it all off. Your scalp gleams. Large eyebrows that fan out above your big, naive, mischievous eyes. I think I'm lucky. But that can be a premature feeling. You brought me a gift. A golden egg. Almost Easter. The egg itself is made of chocolate, wrapped in golden silver foil. Is this a promise? You can hardly look at me. Which is strange. I have a whole day with you.

Naked in the hammock. A bit of jerking off. Falling in love, looking straight into each other's eyes. I tell you that I walked on clouds last week. And how I tried to evaporate the clouds. You also walked on clouds. We both walk on clouds. Mist. It's very misty around us. We only see ourselves. Ourselves. And maybe a piece. A piece of the other. You are. Beautiful. You have a big. Cock. A beautiful body. Chest hair. I want you. Smell you. Smell, hold you. You must never. Never leave again. But you go. Go away. And promise me. Another Friday. Farewell. Farewell, you say. Like you always do. Always saying 'See you in the plum season.' Plum season is a few weeks. A few weeks in August. In August or never.

The weekend is over before it even started. I'm blurrier than ever. Can't imagine feeling what I feel. Is this dull feeling love? That nothing matters except you? I want this for the rest of my life. I want this for the rest of my life. I want this for the rest of my life. I want this for the rest of my life. I want this for the rest of my life.

Thursday, April 20

HELP

TIGER,

I

AM

IN

LOVE

What should I do? Yesterday, I received an email from Maurice. He talked about a crisis in his relationship and a vague situation, mentioning that he's shocked and still in a slump. I don't understand what he's talking about. I know he has this relationship, and every relationship has its crises. How many did we have in those two and a half years? About five? I remember ashtrays flying across the room, you kicking me out, and how we would make up because we simply loved each other too much and couldn't be without each other. But maybe I shouldn't compare his relationship to ours.

Maurice goes on to write that he finds me very nice, sexy, interesting, and horny, but he needs to be careful. He doesn't want to come across as hypocritical, but keeping me a secret makes him feel that way. Additionally, he doesn't want to drive me crazy.

Do you understand any of this? I'm just in love. I don't care if he keeps me a secret or not. It's entirely his business, right? Of course, I hope for him that he can be completely open and honest with his man, but if this unexpectedly isn't possible... What value does that relationship have, I wonder? Am I to blame for his relationship being a farce? I'm completely disheartened and feel ridiculous. Nevertheless, I couldn't resist and immediately replied that I'm madly in love with him and that I have no problem with him having a man with whom he has a lot to figure out. I won't be more or less in love because of it.

What would you do in this situation? Should I demand that he plays his cards openly? I'm not even sure if he's also in love with me. I'm going crazy. I'm finally in love again, and this happens to me. But I will fight for it. Everyone gets what they deserve. I want him and the feeling he gives me. I feel like a young dog just thinking about him. It's as if I have no past. Nothing else matters. I don't care if the whole world collapses now. Of course, I still do the things I have to do, like work and be there for friends. But otherwise, I couldn't care less. Can you imagine that?

I planned not to tell anyone, but to illustrate the urgency; last night, I cycled past his house. In the middle of the night. Around two o'clock. All the lights were, of course, already off. It felt very exciting. I had a lot of fun doing something so absurd. I had to cycle through the park, and I sang loudly. No, I wasn't drunk, and I hadn't smoked either. It was out of pure infatuation that I couldn't keep quiet. For a moment, I thought about starting a ballad in front of his house, but I quickly dismissed that idea as soon as it came up. You know my voice. The song I had in my head was this super kitschy number by John Denver. 'You fill up my senses'. I tried to make a translation of it. I couldn't sleep when I got home.

You fill up all my senses like a night in a forest, like the mountains in springtime, like a walk in the rain, like a storm in the desert, like a sleepy blue ocean.

Ach, die Liebe.

A kiss from the head-over-heels old Wolf

Saturday, April 22

la publicité

Tiger,

I AM THE HAPPIEST MAN ON EARTH

I still can't quite believe it, but yesterday was one of the most fantastic days of my life. Forgive me. I'm trying to be as historical as possible.

I woke up early with an exciting feeling in my stomach, and there was a pleasant buzz around my head. Since it was Friday, and Maurice could come around eleven, I thoroughly showered and groomed myself. I put some thought into what I would wear, at least a red T-shirt. I walked through my room, making sure it was tidy and cozy. To make the waiting easier, I went to get croissants and a newspaper. So, I sat with a cup of coffee reading the newspaper, which was a bit challenging because I haven't had a TV for a while, and I couldn't place everything in the right context.

After thoroughly going through the newspaper, which felt like solving a complex puzzle, I looked at the clock. It was almost twelve. I still hadn't received a response to my love emails from the previous days, and it was still unclear if there would be any response at all. Briefly, anxiety struck, but I ignored it as quickly as possible. I didn't want to lose my feeling of infatuation. I strongly believe that I am the master of my own feelings and can 'steer' them.

But the clock kept ticking, and I started to worry slowly. Maybe I was too quick to express my strong feelings. I checked my mailbox again, but no message from Maurice. I also checked if my phone was fully charged and if I hadn't accidentally overlooked a message. At that moment, it rang. Excitement surged through me when I saw Maurice's name on my display through the ringtone and vibrations. I answered and greeted him warmly and coolly, as I thought it should be. Being too enthusiastic would have been misplaced, and if I had been too distant, I knew what fate would have befallen me.

The conversation went well. It turned out he was cycling. He was near a park. I asked which park, and it quickly became clear that this park was the Westerpark. Maurice was no more than a kilometer away from my house. Within five minutes, he could be in my living room. But I also understood that my house might be a bit too direct for his mood, so I suggested that we meet under the Haarlem Gate. In about ten minutes. He thought that was a good idea, and we hung up.

I can't tell you how much I wanted to run out of my house and hug him, but I decided that it would be much wiser to stay calm. Cool-

headed. If only because the situation might be that he was more confused than I was. Someone had to keep a cool head. With these thoughts in my head, and a few others like 'How does my hair look?' and 'Does this T-shirt really work?' and 'How does my butt look in these pants?' and 'Are my teeth clean enough?', I left my house and started my way to the Haarlem Gate.

They are renovating Haarlem Square, and everything is fenced off, so I didn't have a clear view of the Haarlem Gate. I still had to pay attention to where I walked because the traffic flow changes every day. Luckily, it wasn't too crowded, and I managed to walk along the wall next to the railway line to the traffic lights. There, I had a reasonably clear view of the gate, but it was a side view, so it was impossible to see if I would arrive first or if he was already there.

The latter turned out to be the case. He was sitting on the crossbar of his bike, leaning with his arms on the handlebars, with both legs on either side of the bike on the ground. Immediately, there was an exuberant laugh, and at that moment, I was sure that I wasn't the only one with such strong feelings. For a moment, I was completely disoriented, but I don't think it was visible. We greeted each other with a kiss, and before deciding to take a walk, Maurice noted that there was a new bridge to the island.

An iron emergency bridge because the old seventeenth-century drawbridge needed renovation. I understood that he had passed my house a few times, but apparently, he didn't have the guts to ring the bell. I didn't immediately place it, thought back to the day before yesterday when I cycled past his house, and put a note in my head that it made him charming. I held back from telling him that I cycled past his house in the middle of the night.

Thus we walked a bit awkwardly through the old part of the park. Maurice had left his bike under the gate. It is going to be a great spring. The winter lasted a little longer than usual. According to Eric, who has an allotment with his husband, spring is two weeks late this year, and it seemed like this was the moment for nature to burst into full force. A clear blue sky above us and the trees in full bud.

This first bit of park we were making a little conversation. This and that. Small talk. But when we reached the new part of the park, the conversation had taken up speed, and I could finally tell him straight to his face that I was madly in love with him. 'Really?' he asked, and I confirmed it once again. I noticed that my head had detached itself from my neck, that's how high I felt, and I didn't like that he didn't immediately declare his love to me. I didn't doubt it. If someone is so strongly drawn to something, there can be no misunderstanding, *right? I thought that maybe it would be difficult for him to confess his love for me because he's in a relationship. Or maybe he's the type of guy who doesn't easily express his feelings. I decided to keep quiet and keep the conversation going. In the meantime, I searched for ways to hear the decisive words from his mouth. But how?*

I decided to find out what his relationship looked like. Maybe they agreed to be monogamous, and any reference to something else was excluded, and Maurice was in the greatest transgression. Not only towards his friend but especially towards his own identity, morals, principles. A tricky situation, as you can understand. Maybe I'm the first person for whom Maurice has such intense feelings during this relationship.

Maurice told me about a Sunday when he was having a beer with his friend, Bas, as I didn't dare ask before. A guy Maurice had played with before came up to Bas and told him that his friend is very good at making love. It had been quite a hassle for Maurice to quell that crisis. But Bas also had his flings, Maurice told me. There was one now that Bas said was just about sex. As a couple, Maurice and Bas haven't had sex for quite some time, but Maurice noticed that there was a lot of regularity in their contact. They had an argument about it last Tuesday.

You understand that this delicate topic did not leave me. I didn't want to insist on knowing every detail, but I wondered how two people could still stay together despite such jealous tension. In our time, didn't we just have lovers alongside our relationships? Did it matter for our original feelings for each other? I have the idea that having those lovers brought us much closer together. I remember well how much I admired you when you told me that you loved me so much that you wanted to set me free. To be who I was. Precisely because I was who I was, you loved me. And just because I can be who I am, I still love you now. It's that simple in the end, right? If you start judging love by the pain it causes you, life becomes a funeral march. And that can't be the intention of something as fantastic as love, can it?

Explaining this to Maurice was quite a challenge. I began to understand that, for this man, head and heart were very much separated. By now, we had reached the forgotten part of the park behind the railroad. Maurice found great amusement in the name of a meadow to the right of the road. A wooden sign read: Rough play area.

We entered the area, and it turned out to be muddy. I was momentarily worried that Maurice might hesitate to go further, fearing the difficulty of explaining mud on his shoes upon returning home. However, he boldly persevered.

Towards the back of the area, under the trees, it was finally time for a kiss. Both of us kept an eye on our surroundings because two guys making out in a field is not something you see every day, and a passerby might get stuck on the sight. But the kiss was so delightful that I ceased to care about anything else. When we noticed that the kiss was awakening other parts of our bodies, we stopped. If there had been a secluded spot, we would have certainly continued, but on the first truly sunny day of the year, the risk of an unsuspecting walker was too great, it seemed we realized. We took the ferry to the other side of the small water, to what turned out to be an island, and with joyful leaps, we crossed the swaying bridge back to the mainland.

On the other side of the road is a cemetery. Saint Barbara. It's a Catholic cemetery, and its location, between the railroad tracks and the highway, has something special about it. During the time when I was contemplating suicide, I wanted to be buried here. There's a chapel, very small, with a Scandinavian feel, probably because it's made of red stone and you can see the wooden structure. A beautiful simple structure with a kind of roundabout in front, so the hearse doesn't have to turn around. Behind the roundabout begins the garden, and although it's a relatively small area, the space has been optimally utilized. It's divided into sections with hedges around them and paths in between, along which there's a row of trees. Truly a paradise, if you ask me. It's also super quiet there. Maurice and I sat on a bench for about fifteen minutes, overlooking a yellow organic waste container. It was hard for me to imagine that he and I had actually just recently met, so familiar it felt. We went to look at some tombstones. Those Catholics really love their ornaments. Sometimes original, sometimes terribly ugly, but mostly very refined. Those 19th-century angels, you know. I realized that, although I wanted it to be different, this afternoon wouldn't last forever and suggested having a glass of wine on the terrace at West Pacific. On the way there, I couldn't contain myself anymore, and near the petting zoo, I asked Maurice if he was in love with me or not. He replied that he was absolutely in love with me.

A stream of thoughts started that I couldn't quite follow. He told me that he would like to see me at least every Friday, and maybe, if his schedule allowed, more often. He was thinking about Wednesday nights. On that night, he always sleeps in Amersfoort because Wednesday evening is the rehearsal night for his theater group, and the next morning he has to be early at the hospital where he works, also in Amersfoort. From now on, I will be his secret lover.

Can you follow that? I have never experienced anything so bizarre, and I find it amusing. But it is strange. I remarked that the only thing that could stand in the way of our love was his head, and maybe we should just cut it off. He found that thought amusing too, but I don't think he really understood what I meant by it. But well, if he finds it exciting to give our relationship – because that's what it is with such a title, although it doesn't give me any power – that name, so be it. Maybe after some time, when everything becomes a bit clearer and it turns out that our love can overcome everything and what we have together is really cool, we can take off the 'secret' from the title. Although, to be the lover. Do I have it in me to be belittled in such a small-minded way? Apparently so. Because I didn't protest vehemently.

So, we sat for a while by the canal, overlooking the road to Haarlem. Maurice began talking about Bas and the life he has with him. They have been together for three years. Next week, the laptop will be delivered, and today Bas is picking up his new lease car. Maurice pointed out the car to me as it passed by. Of course, without Bas in it. A Volkswagen Passat. Black. I thought the car he pointed out resembled a funeral car. He couldn't laugh about it. He asked me what my ideal car was. I told him about my dreams of driving an orange Saab convertible. He immediately got excited. He had one! From his birth year. 1979. It was a fantastic car, but it fell apart. Maurice likes to speed. Hence. This lease car isn't very nice, he admitted; it even has a cargo bed in the back. A family car. Practical. Maurice made a pained face at that last word. I didn't inquire further. We had to go again. Our encounter came to an end.

You would say that this was my day, but when I got home, another surprise awaited me. I had a message from Belgium. One of my short stories that I had sent to literary magazines will be published. My writing career has started! I immediately called all my friends with the two joyous pieces of news, and everyone was happy for me. Jaco was just 'braaiing chicken' and invited me over. Riding my bike to him felt like I was floating. What if someone could see me now? I counted my blessings. I have the man I want, and as the cherry on top, I am being published! Together with Jaco, I got stoned, and in the middle of the night, I cycled home to fall into a very content sleep.

Today, I am a new person. It's indeed strange not to have the man I'm in love with by my side, but before you know it, it'll be Friday again, and in the meantime, I'll surely manage to email, text, call. Perhaps on Wednesday, I'll take the train to Amersfoort to surprise him, book a hotel, and fuck like there's no tomorrow.

I don't know how, but I'm sending you all the love you can handle! Kisses from the old Wolf

How we stumbled upon each other, how we maintained contact, and how the flames of passion ignited. Countless text messages, love confessions, and stolen kisses on a bench at Saint Barbara amidst angels and conifers. Friday. In essence, there's not much to narrate when you're head over heels. You're simply floating, that's all. Little did I grasp the fortress of certainty you had erected around yourself and how inflexible you truly are. I'm a kind of transgression in your thoughts, while you signify my deliverance. Once you've found me. The Prinsengracht is an extended canal. An eerie ambiance swiftly envelops us. Inebriated, we navigate our way to my abode. This is a dicey situation. I playfully dub you a fool. An endearing term, but I doubt you catch its nuance. Uncertainty isn't exclusive to me in this scenario. Both of us find ourselves in my living room. I prepare a cup of tea and roll another joint. You unleash a tirade against the man you've been entwined with for three years. Three years, you assert, is more than sufficient. According to you, he's overly materialistic. My understanding falters as I'm unfamiliar with him. I yearn to unravel more but am unsure about the trajectory of my inquiries. You, so resplendent. Yet, so awkward. And so recklessly unguarded. I find you endearing. I love you. We decide to cease dissecting it. You follow your heart, and I jestingly label you a fool. A tad disheveled, you scrutinize my room with an intense gaze. Our touches have lost the organic ease of yesterday. Chaos reigns, and we are right in the midst of it. Let's retire to bed. I make love to you with utmost sincerity. I continue to express my ardent affection for you. A nauseating feeling overtakes me, a sense of pathetic self-indulgence. Dizzying, as I now possess everything. Especially you. But for how long? You climax without manual intervention. I comprehend the ramifications of my actions. I desire you. The reason eludes me, yet I'm compelled to unravel your essence. Even if you were detrimental to me, inflicting harm, battering me – I remain indifferent. I yearn to be with you, to endure with you. I'd willingly assume the role of a devoted canine, incessantly licking your heels, bestowing pleasure upon you at your whim, rather than face existence without you. It must be a torment. To acknowledge your existence but remain incapable of kissing you, embracing you, inhaling your essence. I wish to fathom the depths of your being. I want to unravel it all – your most clandestine musings, your anxieties, your dreams. I'm determined to offer solace when needed, to venerate you anew each passing day. To perpetually have you by my side. I am indifferent to the potential repercussions. I would intentionally subject myself to profound unhappiness with you, deliberately misconstruing it as bliss. Not feigning happiness but categorizing it as such. For happiness, after all, is a concept one defines for oneself.

Sunday, April 23

Such a day

Dear Tiger,

Things can change so quickly. Just yesterday, I was still completely torn up from the day before, and yet last night brought another twist. I'm not exactly sure how to deal with it yet. Right now, I'm waiting for a locksmith.

Maurice just left. He was here last night. Not officially, and yet kind of. He had broken up with Bas the night before. Now, he's on his way to a friend's place to recover from the shock, and then he's going to talk to Bas. Maybe he'll be mine again tonight.

That is if he ends his relationship because, as certain as it seemed last night, you never know how things will unfold. Given that I've been pigeonholed without asking for it, even the liberation from the title 'secret lover' is likely to be complicated. Maurice is a bit like a dodgy used car salesman. I don't know why I'm writing it like this. I'm way too excited to worry. I'll try to keep it short.

I spent yesterday daydreaming. Exercised, wrote, and later had a drink at Spijker. Onno was there and asked if I wanted to go to Berlin. I said yes. Berlin is amazing, isn't it? Then I walked a

*bit clumsily along the canal towards home. All
by myself, with all my luck.*

*Maurice called. Turns out he was on his bike
with a bag strapped to the carrier. Of course, he
didn't say he was on his way to me, but I felt like
I had to invite him. So, the man I'm so in love
with cycled to the spot on the canal where I
was. It took ten minutes. In those ten minutes, I
had already gone through all possible scenarios.
How my life would be if he moved in with me
immediately. How my life would be if he didn't
move in immediately but remained in love. How
my life would be if he moved in, and everything
turned out to be a big mistake. I also had
thoughts about Bas, whom I don't know, but
suddenly felt connected to. How would he react
to the sudden departure of his buddy, and in
what awkward position would I find myself if it
became clear how everything had happened?
This impulsive move by my beloved was an
incredibly intense attack on the lives of three
people. Time for a strategy.*

*We walked to my house together. Maurice was
really confused. Nervous. I suspected he rarely
found himself in the state I saw him in. He told
me about his evening. They had gone to the last
Furball with some of Bas's friends. It exploded,
and they had a fight. Maurice told me how he
could now only see the incredibly materialistic
side of Bas. I figured it was probably Bas who
paid the mortgage and got the company car and*

bought the laptop and everything that made life pleasant. With my income, I often don't make it past the second week of the month, and a hospital counselor won't be earning too much either. As I had discovered myself, there's no money in theater unless you direct prestigious operas or ballets.

Maurice's nervousness transferred to me. I tried to remain steadfast and brave and give him a sense of protection, but everything in that direction failed. Even a kiss meant for his mouth ended up behind his ear.

Arriving at my front door, the key broke in the lock. "What could this mean?" Maurice said, and it struck me unpleasantly. Suddenly, I didn't feel like the safe haven where the refugee gets a night's shelter, but as if quality control was being exerted on me to see how well I could fulfill my role. With a bit of pressure, I managed to turn the key and open the door. It didn't feel like a victory.

So, we lay in bed. Me on top. I could think of nothing else but how in love I am with him. This could be the last time we lay in this position, or maybe—and that prospect worried me more— the first time of a long series that ends in boredom.

This morning, we woke up a bit groggy. I made coffee, and in the hammock we discussed how the day would unfold. Bas had called twenty-four times, Maurice sent him a text saying he was still alive. He also called a friend he wanted to talk to about everything, to figure out what choices he should make.

That was two hours ago. I sent him a text with the word 'sucker.' Maybe I shouldn't have. I hope the locksmith comes soon and that Maurice lets me know tonight how everything went.

Kisses from the old Wolf in suspense

Monday, you send me a message. You've made a choice. You kiss me everywhere. You want to be with me but know that it will confuse you again. Or so you think. You need to act normal. For whom, really?

The sun hasn't fully set yet; there's a heavy atmosphere, heavy light. Everything is glowing in the fading sunlight. This is actually the time of day that appeals to me the most. The twilight zone between day and night. You need to act normal. For whom, really?

For a long time, I thought I'm someone else at night than during the day. It can't be any different. Everything changes in the dark. The light, the sound, scents, thoughts. I love changes. I'm always the first one to want to change. Everything always changes. Not a moment is the same. Today is a vacuum. Now is a sealed moment. Forever. You need to act normal. For whom, really?

I enjoy accompanying your thoughts, but I don't know the contents of your head. You don't have to apologize for Saturday. Everything feels like it couldn't have happened any other way. You need to act normal. For whom, really?

I am as electrically charged as I only think of you. I don't entirely understand the backdrop in which you act your play. I do know that you don't need to be afraid to be who you are. Freedom is not a cage. You need to act normal. For whom, really?

Time to become desperate. I am still head over heels. Hormones raging through my body. Unstoppable. Ferocious. It's not about choosing. Quite the opposite. You shouldn't choose. I am not the rival of your husband. Your husband is not my rival. I am not your secret lover. We are in love. There's nothing more. The gap between thinking and feeling. Being sensible. Suddenly, I find myself in a prudish, bourgeois play. You need to act normal. For whom, really?

Do I start to doubt if you are sincere? I refuse. I just keep going. This situation is not my choice. You choose. I get the result thrown in my face, like a wet towel against my head, thrown, kicked. Defeated without knowing what the game was.

If you choose certainty and so much more, why can't you tell Bas that you're in love with me?

Friday, April 28

It's over

Dearest Tiger,

I don't want to talk about it, but I have no choice. I am completely disoriented. This entire Friday has turned into a disaster, and really, the whole week before that too. I feel awful, want to die, or better yet, just disappear. What impossible days. Against my better judgment, I'm trying to hold it together, but today my head exploded, and my heart jumped out of my chest. You know how scientists describe love as a temporary increase in dopamine production. I now feel my body abruptly stop making dopamines. If only I had never fallen in love. If only I had restrained myself. Why can't I ever keep myself in check?

Thank you for your encouraging words and warnings. You're not the only one who warned me. I feel bad for ignoring everyone's advice. Am I even worth being your friend? Everything is so clear, so recognizable, and yet I walk into it like a blind dog. The fool, that's me. That much is clear.

Yesterday, I had plans with Jason. That meeting had been planned for a while. I told him that I was too in love to have sex with him. Strangely, that piqued his interest even more, and he wanted to know everything. Actually, yesterday seemed promising. I even told Foekje that I'm in love with a man I can barely keep up with. She called and wants to visit in two weeks. She has those cards that allow you to travel freely once every six months. I agreed, even though I don't know what the situation will be like by then. At least we can go to the Remembrance of the Dead ceremony on Dam Square. She's never done that, and since it's on TV every year, it might be a nice outing.

Today, with my stupid head, I sat in Vondelpark with my laptop. It was the worst miscalculation in my life so far. After Sunday, which I've extensively reported to you, I received a text from Maurice on Monday afternoon. It was a ceasefire, he wrote, and he deliberately didn't tell Bas about me. That should do it. How clear can someone be? But with my idiotic sense of drama, I decided that this wasn't the end. My feelings are too strong, my life too short, etc.

I decided not to bombard him with messages but wanted to know how things stood. Was he still interested, or was I just a fling to ease the tensions in his relationship? It's tricky when nobody explains anything to you.

It seems that Bas is paying attention to Maurice again. Maurice told me that Bas is finally going to get that job in Milan. Maurice calls this 'a positive development.' It should probably make me feel lenient if a guy loves his boyfriend so

much that he wants to support him in both good
and bad times. If only I had such a relationship.
Maurice let me know that he was grateful that I
embraced him with so much warmth last
Saturday and 'he regretted that he was so
vague.' Furthermore, he informed me that he
was completely confused in my presence and
wondered if this is the effect when two people
are crazy about each other.

I wrote back that the confusion was completely
mutual and that this is indeed the effect that
occurs when two people are crazy about each
other. In the same email, I declared my love to
him once again, unnecessarily, even using the
words 'love.' Given the circumstances, it's
actually unusual, but a desperate person must
do something. Out of respect for Bas, I decided
not to make any comments or questions
towards him or the relationship they have. It's
definitely none of my business.

He even sent me a photo with the caption
'hungover or cute?' I told him both and was glad
I found a man with a sense of humor. In that
photo, he has a very sweet blurry expression in
his eyes, and his ears are great. I have his scent
in my head. But today. I was already awake at
eight out of pure excitement and waited until
nine to write a text. I wondered what we would
do today. Whether he would come for breakfast
or lunch, or if we were just going for a coffee.
He replied that he was too busy, which I found a

bit abrupt, and apparently so did he, because shortly after, he called to explain in detail that he had been asked to write a piece for a prestigious festival in Utrecht and that it was important that he had to work on it. It sounded to me like the most pretentious excuse, and in turn, I told him that I had to make corrections to my short story today. An editor had changed a few things in my text and made suggestions. Nothing substantial, mind you. Just a list of things to make my text 'flow better.' I was now expected to look at these corrections and respond to the changes. I realized that working in the laptop era doesn't necessarily mean working from home, and since Maurice also has a laptop since this week, I suggested that we sit somewhere in the city with our work. Strangely enough, he didn't think it was a good plan. But I had it in my head, and half an hour later, I was in the tram with my laptop, heading to the Blauwe Theehuis in the middle of Vondelpark, within walking distance of his house.

I felt a bit like a devil, but he who does not dare does not win. I positioned myself prominently on the terrace and ordered a coffee while I sent Maurice a text: 'Sitting at the Blauwe Theehuis. The coffee is somewhat drinkable, and the view is not bad.'

What happened next is difficult to explain. It felt like a sledgehammer hit my solar plexus. I felt incredibly restless in an entirely serene environment as I started the corrections to my short story. It took a while before I got a message back. That he was sorry, but it wasn't possible. Now it became clear to me. He had decided not to see me anymore but wanted to keep the possibility open.

I thought I was going crazy.

Felt betrayed, taken for a ride, dancing naked through the streets while the crowd laughed at me. The reserve love. The man who might come in handy, somewhere in the future. Feelings that must be suppressed because the head rules.

I wanted to jump behind the bar and eat all the cleaning tablets from the coffee machine at once. I wanted to hang myself with a rope from a tree. I wanted to lay my head on the tram rails. I wanted to sink into the terrace and leave the city through the groundwater. On the contrary, I stood up, left the terrace, went inside, and ordered another coffee. I let Maurice know that I wasn't interested in this and that it should just be over.

Another blow. I could swear that I felt what he should be feeling. I imagined him cursing and screaming through his house, standing outside, on his way to me, but restraining himself, and, upon re-entering, throwing a coffee mug against the wall.

If he can be so expressive.

Tried for another hour to focus on the corrections of the story, where the words began to wander before my eyes and fluttered together like moths as if the screen of my laptop were the only source of light in this universe.

On the tram back home, the message came that maybe this was for the best. Damn it.

Jason is coming in a moment. I don't see him often, but it's as if he's drawn to my intense emotions. I think I'm going to let him comfort me, and tomorrow is Queen's Day. I'm pretty beaten up. I think.

Love from the old Wolf

I'm not waiting for stability. I'm flying.

I can't offer you anything. I don't have a career. I don't have a leased car. I don't have money, and I don't own my house. I don't participate. I'm flying.

I don't care about the game. I go without. Completely.

I have to act normal. For whom, actually? But not about the big things. I am who I am and won't deviate from that. Not for anyone. I can't offer you more than uncertainty. And a bit of love. Love is abundant. I'm flying.

Love can be obtained. Not certainty. You say it doesn't matter to you, as long as my heart is rich. I see you hesitate. I have to remember that I'm not flying.

I'm a fool. An idiot. I have to remember that I'm not flying.

Why on earth did I fall in love with you? I have to remember that I'm not flying.

Why was I the one who had to send that message on Friday? I felt completely ridiculous after a week hanging between uncertainty and hope. I have to act normal. For whom, actually?

I AM STARTING TO UNDERSTAND

Reluctantly battling feelings of love. I'm falling.

You had decided you could write to me but not see me.

You send a photo of yourself. What game are you playing, actually?

The way you look. The way you behave. The way you play with your own feelings and mine.

I thought I couldn't do it. Believed that in that case, you might be too much for me. That it wouldn't be possible for me to understand you. To play with you like you're playing with me.

I'm falling.

Why do I keep underestimating myself?

I'm not afraid.

Not for anyone.

Not for you, and certainly not for myself.

Falling.

If there's something I have to discover about myself, and you're going to show me, bring it on!

Falling.

With open eyes and, even if my whole body gives in, as long as I'm not dead—which is actually a contradiction—I will stand and, with your permission, I will fly.

I'm falling. I have to remember that I'm not

falling.

How far will you go? How far do you want to go? Are you willing to risk everything to be able to fall again?

I have to remember that I'm not falling.

Choices I make. Over and over.

I have to remember that I'm not falling. I have to act normal. For whom, actually?

I was born to fight. I have to remember that I'm not falling.

I believe in the honesty of the fight. The strongest wins and honors the other to whom he owes his victory.

I have to remember that I'm not falling.

There is no other way than that of justice. But what is just? No other way than becoming who you are. Maybe I'm getting ahead of myself.

It's just. That my irony is only useful as a cynical remedy for a life full of chances but without an outcome.

It's just. That the goals, in which I believe so little, are the only things that bring peace.

It's just. That you know where you stand.

It's just. That you know where you're going.

It's just. That you know where you're going with your life.

It's just. That what you can't take with you to the grave has value.

Happiness.

Is.

Not.

For sale.

The options. Thursday night. I could go to the park. Gravity has never felt this good.

I can scour all the bars with dark spaces. Gravity has never felt this good.

Maybe visit the night sauna again. Gravity has never felt this good.

Meet someone on a dating site and, in an entirely incomprehensible impulse, cycle halfway through the city to end up with someone who is just as lonely, or maybe even lonelier than I am. What an enticing prospect. I think I'll stay home. Gravity has never felt this good.

No matter how your mind tricks you into denying your heart, you will always have me to deal with. Your dreams will never be the same. Will you look back at the man who wanted so much to be with you that, instead of denying himself, as he would in equal circumstances, became more and more himself. Started to acknowledge himself. Started to recognize himself in your reflection. Gravity has never felt this good.

I think I've lost all my goals. Since I know you, everything has become unimportant. I go to work and play the office slave. But in my thoughts, I am with you. I meet up with friends and patiently wait for the moment when I can talk about you and how fantastic you are, even though everything related to you is shrouded in dubious haze. When I'm home, I don't know what to do with myself out of excitement. I fiddle with unfinished texts. Write love letters to you, try to tackle my brainwaves with my keyboard, try to restrain my urges. I'm not going to call you. I'm not going to send you messages. I'm not begging for love. Although... No. I'm not begging for your love. If you don't want to give it to me, then so be it.

So I'm writing you another message.

I really don't know what to think or do.

Everything seems like too much. When I send you an email, the sentences come naturally, as if I know exactly what to say. As if I'm acting a role in a play I don't know but is so captivating that I can't stop.

I'm playing myself. At the same time, this is the

most natural thing that can happen. It's scary.
I'm too fatalistic. I've watched too many movies,
read too much literature, I was too focused.
What someone is willing to do for their love... I
have to do other things. Like writing and talking
and communicating and researching and
experiencing.

You're not my endpoint. I would like to give you
that honor, but I'm not ready for it yet. Rather,
you're a starting point or come together with
the starting point of who I am and who I will be.

That's a pleasant thought. Maybe we should
never come together. Just be in love and stare
at each other from a distance. Across a wide
ravine. Across a wild river, in which we would
both drown if we tried to come together. Who
says we will be happy with each other? Maybe
—and admit it—there's a greater chance of
unhappiness than happiness. Both you and I are
more impulsive than we want to admit. We seem
to seek difficulties as if we were bored in our
eternal state of survival. As if we are looking for
problems that give our lives meaning.

Tuesday, May 2nd

On choosing

Dearest, cutest,

How was your weekend?

Mine was bizarre. First, Friday with you, and then Jason came by. Ended up fooling around. Saturday, I was unbearable and felt particularly crappy. Got drunk later in the evening and flirted like crazy, but didn't want anyone. Spent the entire day on Sunday with the edited text. Today, I have a cold. Eric, one of my bosses, brought vitamins and Nisyleen, and now I'm sitting with a bowl of noodles in my lap.

I think of you.

Relentlessly. Can't believe it's over. Don't want it to be over. My body refuses to admit that. I deleted all the messages. Am I too stubborn, banging my head against a wall until my brain breaks?

I am a fool. An idiot.

Why on earth did I fall in love with you? Why was I the one who had to send that text on Friday? I felt utterly ridiculous after a week of swinging between uncertainty and hope.

I think I get it, although I haven't heard it from your mouth. Maybe you don't want to talk about it. Are you too busy or do you have something else to do, or are you just a coward?

Do I care? No, not really. Still crazy about you. Want to hold you and kiss you and never think again.

The further away you seem, the more I want you.

Did I say something I shouldn't have? No, I mean everything I say and write, and I won't lie now either.

Maybe you're completely fed up with me, last week already, but I wanted to look around because the view is so impressive.

Maybe you were really busy, not getting worked up like I was. Do I really have such an ego problem?

Maybe I was just a solvent, and as someone occasionally pointed out, it's fine as it is.

Absurd.

It's not fine as it is without you; it wasn't fine as it was with all that silly mysterious stuff. And if it ever gets better, something I firmly believe because I can't imagine you really doing what you say, I'll drag you deep into the jungle and completely ravish you.

Wednesday, May 3rd

Possibilities

Sweetest,

Where are you? Are you still alive? This is never going to work for our epistolary novel. Or do you really not know how to respond to me anymore? No worries. I have no idea either.

I imagine you opening your email. I suspect you're too curious not to read me.

The measure of all things. And how different we are. It's not boring. It's becoming strange. Is this what we meant by fantasizing?

It's challenging that it remains silent on the other side. Maybe also understandable.

I know how I feel, and the quieter it gets, the more I get a sense of you. How you don't let your cards be revealed. How strong you must be to handle this. How foolish I must be to want this.

It's almost unbearable. I am disappointed, casually happy, and ecstatic. Maybe I enjoy my own emotions too much.

Do you hope to shake me off, to let it slide off you by remaining cold? It makes me sad. It's not what I want. And maybe I should indeed stop. Just let you be. Not hold it against you. How could I?

In the end, I can only blame myself for my own enthusiasm. I must stop exposing myself like this. Before you really start to like me.

Kisses wherever you want

Thursday, May 4th

Follow your heart...

Indeed! I won't let myself be beaten down.

Tiger!

New round, new opportunities.

It's a strange, dubious time. Over the weekend, I thought long and hard about what I want and who I am. I tried to follow your advice as much as I could, to be in the now and meditate on what's really going on.

Last Saturday was a mess. I couldn't find peace, and I stayed at the Spijker until closing time on Saturday night. I played the aspiring literary talent and asked various people how to handle a round of corrections for a literary magazine. Suddenly, I find myself in the company of ambitious literati, it seems.

In short, it comes down to this: How much do I want to be published?

If I don't care, then I should interpret my text the way I intended it. Shamelessly leave word for word what I want. It seems that in all language areas except Dutch, what the writer writes is sacred. But because there are too many linguists and literati per square kilometer here, I can forget about that. No matter how good my language is, there will always be people who

know better how I should express myself.
Another option is to accept all corrections
without objection. In that case, I will hardly be
taken seriously because it would seem like I
don't care, and a good writer must have
thoughts about what he writes. Supposedly.
The most manageable solution remains: praise
the editor who proposed the corrections, agree
with most of his or her suggestions, but insist
on a few things that I really cannot let slide. And
that's done. I'll let another week pass before
sending it back, just to be sure. Then, as far as
I'm concerned, the text is free, and I'll also send
it to you.

I've been rehired for a year at the office. I don't
quite understand what I'm doing right there, but
I seem to fit well into the team. I'm not the
sunshine all the time, but I try to be tough. And I
must say that Fred and Eric really suit me. I have
a good life with them, and they told me that I
save them a lot of work. The best thing about
office life is the copious amounts of coffee and
the strange humor that arises when you're in a
room of fifty square meters with three men.

As for my clumsy love, I've decided to go for it. I
sent Maurice two emails about how I feel and
that I still want him. His reaction, I can be brief
about that. He starts his reply with 'All the
sweetest on earth.' That's the short version.

The longer version is that he wants to see me,
kiss me, hold me, and more. That he is charmed

by my messages. That he is consciously and unconsciously suppressing many things and that he wants to work more passionately on his passion. By that, he means the theater. He also says he struggles with distancing himself and finds it difficult that this doesn't penetrate my understanding as quickly. Maybe it's all still in there, but he needs to think carefully about how to acquire it...

So, there is hope. I think.

Only two weeks left, and you'll be here. Are you sure you can stay at Gillis? Lovely, Adrian's house. Is he in Stuttgart that weekend?

I'm going to the station to pick up my mother.

Love from the old Wolf

Monday, May 8th

Raw Fish

Tiger!

Well, Foekje is gone again, and I ended up with a fast bike, a refrigerator, a washer plus dryer, two pants, a shirt, and a toothbrush.

Last week, we went to Dam Square to watch the commemoration. We were there early and had good spots up front. Just before eight, the entire Dutch political elite passed by, along with the royal family. When they rushed past us like a swarm of black ravens, Foekje noticed that Maxima looks very different in person than on TV. But of course, she reasoned, that's because you're not allowed to laugh at the commemoration. I think the problem was the heavy makeup that had been slathered on in thick layers for the live TV broadcast. That always looks a bit strange. Live.

But otherwise, everything was as it should be. Sharpshooters were on the roof of De Bijenkorf, and a girl read a poem she had won a contest with. When the wreaths were laid, the blue blood was escorted away to the back of the monument, and the political elite was loaded onto a bus parked next to the stock exchange. I took my mother to the sushi place on Zeedijk. She didn't like chopsticks, and I managed to get the only fork in the whole place for her. She really likes raw fish, and she had never heard of the combination with soy sauce before. But she enjoyed it.

Say hello to Tristan for me! I look forward to meeting him! Lots of love from the old Wolf

PS Here's the story with the corrections. Enjoy!

Survival

Now while I still can. Now that I want to. Now there is no other way. Over the cobblestones of the alley next to the petting zoo, where the rabbits sit dumb in their cages and the speckled sheep with hanging ears wander among the decorative chickens and the worn-out peacocks, I sneak towards the crane hanging above the water.

I should have done this much earlier. I should never have waited so long. It's a shame that I let myself be held back like this. If only I knew why. Irrational, like falling in love with a leg in the supermarket.

Endless falling. That's what I want. Just falling. To see the horizon climb in the corners of my eyes and then, as I tumble forward, to see it again, but inverted. Hearing the sounds of the city fly by in slow motion. The helplessness that clubs my body numb. The scent of victory swirling through my bloodstream. The earth beneath me splits in two. At least I dig a hole in the ground to get into myself and forget the world. Even if it's just for a moment. That's what I want. Today. This morning.

This summer, the hottest in fifty years, was unnecessary. I hoped I could cling to something other than my humor. Hoped for a depression that never came. Hopeless irony. Pleasure of revenge. Optimistic until my grave. Ha. Ha ha.

Ha ha ha.

I've jumped before this summer. In May. It was good. I loved it. The best remedy against fear. The best applause for a well-played role. The best way to get rid of unwanted spirits. Look, I'm flying!

As you are hoisted up in the cage, your coach gives you a few last instructions. You can choose to listen, but the view gets better as you reach the top, squeaking and creaking. This is the second-best moment. You have to turn around. Stand on the edge of the cage with your arms wide, while your coach counts down. From three. Three seconds to let go, wobbling on the edge, looking around.

In May, I saw the city I hated with all its red roofs and stupid church towers. May the sea flood Amsterdam in all its glory and small-mindedness.

At one, you let yourself fall. Forward. Why they call it jumping, I don't know, maybe it sounds more active. Doesn't matter. It feels good, looks good, and while you're in the motion, you can't think anymore. You can only feel.

Your heart escapes your chest, skipping a few beats, but immediately making up for it with a drumroll in the next moment. You hear it pop in your left ear. Your blood has left your head by now, and your pupils have become larger than your eyes. Black holes covering your corpse-white face. This is the moment. Then, without realizing it, your body recovers, and you are in free fall. Let go and touch air.

Maybe I deluded myself with the thought that fear was for losers. Maybe I thought that having pity was noble. Maybe I dreamed that love would take me back to where I came from. Maybe I only had the illusion of dying when luck turned around.

I had to fall again. I wanted to. June, July, August. I really wanted to, but I forbade myself to go to that hideous piece of land where the crane stood with its back to the city. I was looking for a reason.

There is little heroism in me or my family. Sometimes it feels like something is missing in my genes. None of my ancestors tried to be more than they were. In close-up, no one in my family tried to be someone. How wise. Adapt. Shut up. Do what is expected of you. Even my mother, who burned her bra in her student years and walked through life as a heroine during my childhood, couldn't help herself and convinced me that I needed protection. A rich lesson in certainty.

Today, I have decided to leave all that behind. I am going to jump. I am going to jump, just for the thrill and adrenaline. Push my senses to the limit. Gain control of who I really am. If I keep my mouth shut, it's because I decided to.

Three testosterone bombs stand at the foot of the crane. It looks like they're discussing something. All three wear only shorts. I wait at the counter. One of the men sees me and waves while showing a smile. He is the only one with chest hair. Blonde curls from his neck over his broad chest to circle down to his belly in red and white shorts. He wears a baseball cap on his head. I notice that I smile back, stiffly, with my hands in my pockets. Then he walks to the counter.

"Our first today," he begins cheerfully. "Is that so?" "We've only been open for five minutes, you tell me." "I have that discount voucher." I take out the small pink paper, which had been pinned under the screen of my computer for all those months, and lay it on the table. "Then you know how it works." The man takes out a pink paper from a bag on which the company dodges all responsibility in case I fall to my death while hanging on the elastic. No problem, I skip the tedious legal language and want to sign. The pen doesn't work. The man pulls another pen from the bag. Black.

Dear Mom,

Thank you for all the beauty you have given me. It was a fantastic ride, but now it's over. I hope you will find peace. I love you.

Behind the man, helping me through the paperwork, one of the boys jumps into the water. I see him trying to grab a piece of dark driftwood from the greenish water. He has it, holds it above his head, and with a firm throw, he throws the piece of wood outside the buoys that connect the iron barges, serving as a pier, in a quarter circle with the quay.

"You're going to dip!" "Dip?" "Dunk your head in the water." "Don't think so." "The water is perfect." "Sure." "Are you sure?" "Absolutely." "Can you step on the scale?"

My weight is written on my hand with a green marker. 74. If I want to go to the bench under the crane, empty my pockets, and take off my shoes. From the bench, I see the boy in the water being instructed to fish a plastic bag out of the water. He casually swims towards it, grabs it, takes it to one of the barges, throws the plastic on it, pushes himself out of the water, and walks straight towards me.

"I'm Ryan. I'm going up with you." Ryan is disgustingly beautiful. His sun-tanned skin is wet, his black short hair full of small water droplets that sparkle in the sharp light, large bright blue eyes that look at me, innocently widened, investigating. Dimples in his cheeks when he laughs. 'Dipping, right?' 'I just washed my hair.' I try to avoid Ryan, which is difficult because he helps me put on the harness. He touches me everywhere I don't want to be touched. Beautiful hands with broad fingers. Perfect teeth, perfect body. Six-pack. Warm. Probably twenty, and studying something everyone studies. Communication, economics, or even law. Could easily be on the cover of a glossy or on TV. Nothing more to be done. Ryan works here to be able to jump every day, for sure.

Ryan asks if he should calm me down. I tell him to enjoy the view and count down when we get there. The crane squeaks and groans. We sway a bit in the wind. Silently facing each other. The view is better than in May. I don't know why, but my anger seems to be over. Amsterdam looks fine; just a pile of stones with an occasional tower. A seagull flies by, it doesn't seem to see us, but I follow it as it glides past. It's a really fat one. Ryan looks down, I look past him over the water to the north. The crane has stopped.

"Count." I turn around, arms wide. Great. Three. Feel that wind. Two. Sun sparkles in the water. One. Let. Go. Fall.

Doing dishes. Put on some music. French voice pants in rhythm. Sunday. Maybe exercise and maybe have a drink somewhere. Almost done with the dishes. Just two pans left. The doorbell rings. Through the window, I see a dark blue police van in front of my house. I dry my hands and press the button that unlocks the front door. Two policemen come up the stairs. A tall blonde and a short dark one. If I want to come with them, it's important. What's it about, I want to know. That will come later, says the blonde. I put on my shoes and a sweater. Turn off the music, and before I know it, I'm standing with my face against the wall, my hands behind my back. They are tied together with a sturdy plastic strip.

"This must be a mistake." I am roughly pulled outside by the blonde. The dark one opens the loading door. Five men on the benches on both sides of the cargo space. I am pushed inside, and I recognize David. I was once with David. Until I broke up with him. I just wanted to be alone. Now we sit next to each other in a police van, along with four other men I have seen before, I just don't know where. Maybe we're on our way to an exciting party where orgies are taken very seriously. "How's it going?" "Dunno." "Shut up!" sounds through the mesh. David shrinks. The man opposite me dares not look at me, but I think I know who he is. Two years ago, I was stalked. The phone rang every ten minutes, and when I answered, I heard nothing. Enough to drive you crazy. Until I saw him. He stood in the rain across from my house, phone pressed against his ear. I let him in, and although he was completely shy, he showered, and I gave him clean dry clothes. I haven't seen him since, but the phone calls stopped. Now he's sitting across from me. A dark stain on his pants.

If you think they learn to drive at the police, you're wrong. I don't know where we're going, but it's unlikely that we'll miss a single pothole in the road. In the curves, taken at great speed and always unexpectedly, so that you feel like tipping over, it's almost impossible to stay on the bench. We can't hold on to anything. I don't believe I've ever had such a rough ride.

When we finally stop and the door opens, our journey is not over; we are standing in the middle of an airport, and, as it turns out, we are not the only ones brought here. About a hundred men in total, surrounded by military police in full regalia, black, with balaclavas and machine guns. I now recognize a lot of faces around me. A talk show host, some actors, artists, journalists, politicians.

It starts to dawn on me what might be going on, but it's hard to concentrate with machine guns pointed at me. A man standing not far from me breaks out of the group and walks straight towards one of the policemen. I know who he is, I've seen him on television many times. He was still in parliament a few years ago. Not an impassioned man, but an indestructible policymaker. He ensured that the reinforced anti-terrorism law was passed. The eyes in the balaclava opposite him shift nervously. The machine gun aimed at the former parliamentarian.

"Who gave you this order?" No answer. "I want

to speak to your superior." The policeman takes a step back. "I demand an explanation." A series of short shots. The politician collapses. We are stunned and watch. Don't look. Don't look.

In the sky above us, night is approaching, large purple clouds slowly drifting towards the horizon. I don't understand what I'm doing here. Why I have to experience this. Were we always the others? We were always different. I stare patiently, but extremely tense, upwards. If we are all shot down soon, let me be the first.

From behind the hangar in the distance, a cargo plane taxis in. The large machine looks like a lame big bird. Still royal. Still incredibly blue. As it rolls towards us, we are driven even closer together than we already are. My hands hang against someone's crotch, and I smell the fear sweat of my right neighbor, who with drooping shoulders looks despondently in the direction of the plane. Maybe we're not going to die yet. Maybe we're being taken somewhere where we have to work hard for the rest of our lives. Will we be beaten if we just look at each other and put on a diet of mashed sprouts.

We have to enter the plane at the back. The hatch is lowered, and we obediently let ourselves be pushed into the dark hole where, if we can't go any further, we are told to sit on the ground. Beaten down is more the word. I manage to sit on my hands. They are quite numb and cold. When we're all inside, the hatch closes. Four rotating blue lights on the ceiling steadily turn their blue circles. The plane starts to move, and the policemen on board strap themselves to their seats, their machine guns clutched close to them.

Usually, I sit by the window. I want to stare at the flat land during takeoff. See the sharp shadow of the plane beneath me fade in the meadows. Cycle behind the clouds until the dike stops the land, and I see the wet sand between me and the island across turn red in the setting sun on top of the basalt blocks. The electricity wires hang heavily between the iron poles that disappear into nothingness. The silver ditches that cut off the green squares with a clump of bushes here and there. Cows curiously running after you. Old men discussing world politics on fences in the middle of nowhere. The best time to spread manure over the land. The horny wife of the doctor who hangs her laundry outside on Sundays.

The sizzling air during haytime. A swaying row of tall trees, the poplar leaves that keep rustling and whispering endlessly in the cool night, the moon rising above the mist, the northern lights. The tractor that passes by at four in the morning. The rooster that wakes everyone up and turns out to be too tough, even for the soup.

According to my time estimation, not accurate, as I daydream, we've been hanging in the air for about half an hour. It has become chilly in the belly of the plane. Everyone around me is languid. Silent in the humming sound of the engines. Invisible in the strobe light. We're there and yet not quite. I discreetly shift, allowing my bound hands to come out from under my legs. Hidden behind a tall, broad back, I slowly maneuver first one leg and then the other through my arms. With effort, I manage to wriggle my right hand free.

TL beams flash on. The policemen jump up and shout at us. We should stand. Panic. Try standing up with your hands tied behind your back. The hatch opens. A cold, thin wind rushes in, and the policemen start pushing us out of the plane. "Jump, damn it, jump!" The TV presenter nearby gets hit with the butt of a machine gun. Iron hits him on the chin. Blood splatters from his mouth. We are forcibly ejected from the plane. I weave my way through the men blocking my path. Just a little more. I see the horizon where the sun has set. Someone stumbles in front of me. I manage to avoid him. Five big steps. I stretch out my arms. Go. Fall. Free.

II   STRATEGY OF THE WOLF

Thursday, May 11

The alarm goes off with the sound of a crashing plane. I was just sleeping so soundly. Dreaming. I stand in a black plowed field with an enormous, razor-sharp sword. Heads of unknown men emerge from the ground, and I swing my sword, cutting them off one by one. With each rolling head, blood sprays into the ash-gray sky like a fountain. In the distance, flags flutter amidst the smoke of burning farms. I open my eyes. It's Thursday, I realize immediately, and roll to the edge of my bed, reaching out to the alarm clock just far enough to stretch. I grope on the left side of the glowing digital letters until I find the two buttons I need to push upward. It takes me the second attempt. I roll back onto my back. Look at the ceiling. This is the third time this month I've had this dream. Does it mean something?

I need to get up. Come on, out of bed! With a nimble twist, I stand at the foot of my bed and turn on the light. Through the narrow passage to the kitchen, where I make coffee first. Shower. Back through the passage. Second door on the right. Light switch on the outside. A mirror covering the entire wall in front of me. I look into it. Shit, completely forgot. The right side of my face is paralyzed.

This is not convenient. I try to stretch the skin with my hands, but nothing happens. The muscles are paralyzed, numb, and without sensation. Damn.

It started yesterday morning. During work, I felt as if I had just been to the dentist. The days before, nothing tasted as it should. Suddenly I remember. I feel it again, as if a knife is being pressed between my ribs. A blow to my midriff. I'm still in love. Just so you know.

Nothing from you again. Logical, because you only read your emails at work, and you've had the flu since yesterday. I briefly thought I might have infected you, but we did everything safely. The only way to get something is to let it go. Then it will come looking for you. If it's in the cards.

I'm starting to hate my phone. It's only been a month, but I've spent so many empty hours staring at the screen that I can dream the font and how the words fill the screen. Fortunately, I'm wise enough to delete all messages when it all gets too much.

Maybe I should pull up the blinds. With a firm pull, I see a train coming to a halt in front of my house. I see the sleepy commuters staring over the gray noise barrier. When I first moved here, that noise barrier didn't exist. I used to sit for evenings on end on a stool, watching the passing trains. I didn't have blinds back then. The noise barrier doesn't stop the sound, doesn't make it less, and it doesn't matter. There's something about having a railroad in your front yard.

The trees on the other side of the railroad are in full leaf. Strange how quickly summer has come this year. One week it was still hailing, and a week later, it was twenty degrees.

My mother told me that the chestnut tree was cut down by the new owners. I planted it as a four-year-old next to the farmhouse, and in thirty years, it had grown into the strongest and tallest tree on the property, with huge yields of sweet chestnuts collected by my nephews and then warmed by my brother in an old oil drum. The past never comes back.

If the weather is going to be really nice today, maybe I shouldn't stay in the office too long. Maybe I can use my face as an excuse, even though it doesn't hurt. On the contrary, the right side is completely paralyzed. Numb. I already know what the jokes will be. I'll say that I'm going to do the left side of my face next week. Left, for the viewers, right.

On my bike, I always take the Keizersgracht. If I walk, it's the Prinsengracht. I know that street like the back of my hand. Know where the light changes as the canal curves around the city. The Westerkerk church is the midpoint of the route. I'm walking today. By feeling. The trees along the canal. Green lifts. Over water. Houseboats bob. Calm. No rush. I walk more often. Know every step. Exactly half an hour.

You should be at work now. Your first meeting. Your first coffee. Your first cigarette. How do those things work in a hospital? In Amersfoort. An hour by train. I miss you. Never had you. Longing. Something that cannot describe itself.

A nice bum. I love nice bums. To follow. Like a dog, I am. I follow until it crosses the canal toward the Jordaan. Light bounces off the facades. Red. Yellow. Orange. Houses from a fairy tale. Houses in Amsterdam. Amsterdam, a fairy tale. In the morning. Maybe.

Anne Frank is busy. Early. Asia. Middle East. America. Germany. Italy. Shiny iron railing to protect everyone. Everyone knows where the writer lives. Today. Everyone knows where she lived.

Opposite her, next to the bridge, lies an old barge. The barge of an Englishman. A tattered mattress. A rickety kitchen. Charity. When I used to be charitable. Or very insecure. Or that I didn't know. Or that I didn't care anymore. Or that I needed attention. From strangers. A bit of everything. A lot of everything. The Englishman had red hair and ears like sails. The old barge is rotting away in the water opposite.

How many? I don't remember how many there are. How many? I don't know which number you are. How many? If that number exists. How many? Everything is calculable, and if not, there's probably a formula for it. How many? To know where and how and how many. Lost count. I knew it. I knew it when I was seventeen, then it became vague. Impossible mathematician. How many? Sex like mathematics. Coincidence like fate. Numbers like rain. How many? You're my number one. I just keep thinking. Only about you. I should stop that. I should stop it. If only I knew how. To stop. How?

The Rozengracht is busy. Three trams pass each other. Cars avoid cyclists. Cyclists avoid pedestrians. Pedestrians avoid taxis. As if it's always been like this. Green. I cross. Everyone stops. That's how it should be. An old man drinks coffee on a wicker chair on the corner. My name is Frank. I'm always called Frank. Drama. Frank is not to be trusted. I'm not to be trusted. Today is today and tomorrow is tomorrow, and everything that comes after that, I don't know yet, and everything that came before, I've lost. Just like you. I don't know who you are. If only I knew myself, then I'd know a lot. I know nothing. Only that I want to be with you, for no good reason. For no simple calculation. For no purpose. Just to be with you. Where are you?

Autumn. Wet. The air is rotten. Leaves in soggy heaps on the side of the street. Leaves on the bottom of the canal or on their way there. On the top floor of the society that used to be the center. Forget it. As long as you don't beat me up or give me a dirty look or spit on the ground in front of me or call after me as if you knew me and played a prank on me. Up there on the top floor, we practiced for months. A director with a passion for Eastern European whores. His pencil assistant, bespectacled with jam jar glasses, who behaved like an accomplice. The graceful Brazilian who lived in New York but couldn't get a green card and therefore traveled back and forth. No one knew why or for what purpose, and he dodged all questions with a kind of typical ironic mysterious tact that made you afraid to ask further.

And we kept playing. Three Dutch people in English. 'It sounds really natural.' Something about a Czech whore who wants to marry a client, but the nasty, shit-craving pimp Frank, me, puts a stop to it. A row of taxis patiently awaits hotel guests who are pushed onto the road by two porters in shiny red uniforms, still drunk and stoned from the previous night. I patiently step around the wheeled suitcases. I once got lost in this hotel. And the quickie was disappointing too.

What do you think of me? I just wondered. Did I fall from the sky for you too? Were you also completely surprised? Is inexperience the reason you're so slippery?

A few more steps, and I'm at the gate of the alley that leads to my work on the attic floor of the garden house. I insert the key into the lock and climb the spiral staircase. I'm the first one today. Fred is in Switzerland, and Eric won't be here until ten.

We deal with communication. Today, I'm going to fill envelopes with booklets that I'll push into mailboxes. Odd jobs. But first, I read my email. Drink coffee. Check my phone. Your last message. The one about being a limp dishcloth. How you should lie in your bed. Probably now back in a rabbit sleep with strange feverish dreams. How your head sweats on your pillow, and the sheets wander around your body like in a Renaissance fresco. Beautiful naked man. Delete.

I rarely do anything under duress. Never, actually. I force myself or something in me forces me; I never know how to describe it. The word passion is too limited, and focus is something I reserve only for men like you. Delete.

When my face started to sag, you wished me good luck in the doctor's waiting room. Delete.

I don't know anymore. I want to get everything in order, but no matter what I try, it seems impossible. Am I too stubborn? Are you too obstinate? It's going to be something if we manage to start something together. Delete.

One by one, the envelopes slide into the red mailbox. Opposite, on the other side of the canal that intersects the Prinsengracht at a right angle, lives a boy. On the ground floor. At number four. Wannafuckass. Recognizable by sneakers and jeans and everything in between. He's been asking for two months when I'm going to visit. I keep saying tomorrow. Tomorrow never comes.

I walk over the bridge and peek inside Wannafuckass's place. It's dark. He's probably at work, just like me. Heavy curtains and flower pots with cacti. I know what it looks like inside. He has photos on his profile. Poses in the middle of his living room. In white joggers. Next to a couch with rags. In front of a palm tree. Bare feet on a dark wooden floor.

I would be lying if I said I wasn't looking. To be honest, I started my search the week before I met you. The last time I was officially with someone was three years ago. Delete.

In the windows of the gym where I used to do my workouts a few years ago, but not anymore because you can only buy continuous subscriptions, I see myself walking. I need to do something about my hair. It's too long, and now that half of my face is drooping, it looks sad. Luckily, only my face is affected, and the rest of my body is fine. Actually, I'm in top shape. I've never looked so good, apparently others think so too because I've never had so much attention in the last few months. Maybe I can see better now, or maybe I have less trouble with who I thought I was. It seems I'm a lot more complicated than I look.

The Johnny Jordaan Square. Four bronze musicians stand next to a brightly painted house, entertaining the crowd. I'm pushing the remaining envelopes into the mailbox. The terrace on the corner is full. I forgot to put on my sunglasses. My right eye can hardly take it. Everything faded. Tears. I got eye drops. I have to be careful. Since it might take a while for it to recover, there's a risk of dehydration. Dehydration means loss of vision. I already feel so blind. Lunch.

Eric and I sit across from each other. He observes me thoroughly. I always feel a bit uncomfortable when he does that. He's not one for a casual glance. I burst into laughter. It must look strange because I see a big shock, if only for a moment.

"What did the doctor say exactly?" "That it's herpes in the nerve pathway." We each spread a slice of bread. "He gave you antivirals?" "Yes. I was thinking of trying acupuncture.' 'Then wait a bit with that." "Why?" "So you can measure the effects. If you start trying other things alongside the medications now, you won't know what helped afterward. Or if you suddenly get a weird rash, then you won't know the culprit." "I've never heard of a weird rash after acupuncture." "By way of example." "Maybe you're right."

I try to keep a piece of bread in my mouth. For this, I have to press the right corner of my mouth closed with my hand. This additional action is also necessary when I drink. The action is less thorough. Just a guiding finger to keep my lower lip up. Enough. Outside. I light a cigarette. Luxurious, empty day. The canal is the canal. I can go left or right. Maybe I should just go home and lie down a bit. Maybe I should look at shop windows in the Jordaan and get a coffee at Andrew's. Maybe it's time for white wine with Vincent. Maybe I should drown myself in the canal now that our love seems so devoid of perspective. I turn right and walk straight. The sun is now above the canal. This part still has bollards. Half an hour. Then I'll be home.

I have to erase you out of my system. And quickly. Misfortune will befall me if I don't. I have to write down everything I know about you. And I have to write down everything I know about myself. And I have to stop thinking. And stop feeling because it all serves no purpose. Just reflections of reflections of reflections. Before I go crazy, I need to know who you are and who I am and who we would be together. Delete.

I have to be careful not to be too much in my head. It should also be no surprise that the right side of my face is disabled. My left hemisphere is overheated. I can't think normally anymore. It's not a surprise. I am desperate. In love. Delete.

I've thought about not seeing you; you lie shivering in your bed, and the right side of my face goes out. God has humor, that's for sure.

If you're reading this, you're undoubtedly feeling better; I'm sitting here with an eye that won't close and a mouth that's better off not laughing.

Above all, I have to keep my head cool. But how? I exaggerate so easily. Am so easily inflamed. Want so much, so quickly.

While I. While I actually. While I'm actually a freewheeler. Someone not to be caught. I slip through all nets. Jump over all fences. Dive behind all bushes. I know no fear. I am it. A person like me shouldn't be afraid. I am not afraid. Of nothing. Doesn't fit the image. Of myself. Of the people I'm with. Of the world I live in. Everything is free. Everything is open. If I sound too idealistic, you should hit me.

And this too shall pass. Praise the day when I will no longer think of you. Praise the day when we are rid of each other. After the last time, I thought I would remain alone forever. That I am not fit to go through life with someone. Delete.

I was alone for a long time. I introduced myself as the eternal bachelor. As the lonely cowboy who rode towards the sunset every day. As the free man you want but can't get. How painful that the man who can get me doesn't want me. Delete.

But I won't linger in my complaints. The day is far from over, and before it is, I will have taken my first steps on the path to the solution. It just can't be any other way. The wind of change blows at any moment. Nothing stays the same. Not what I think, not what I feel, not who I am.

The hammock is gone. I lay in it too much, and I felt like it started to stink.

Almost three hours, and I'm just staring at myself in the mirror. Watching how my face sags. How my eye sags. How my heart sags.

Where is my camera? Before my hair comes off, I'll capture how it was when there was no turning back. I can't convince you. Trust in a good outcome. Do you trust me? Delete.

Too much daylight seeps through the windows. I lower the blinds and close them. There's only one facial expression somewhat acceptable for me today. That expression is called expressionless. That's how people prevent wrinkles. Simply never use the muscles in your face. My right side is almost completely smooth. I have to practice not to laugh. I always laugh. Almost always. Not necessarily because I'm so cheerful. Often just for approval. Or for a good feeling. Or to avoid friction. From today, I won't laugh until my muscles work again. I grasp my face with both hands. Feel the areas of my face. The left side feels normal. The right side, numb flesh.

The little camera has seen me in all positions. I'm not reserved when it comes to capturing myself. I play with the camera, the light, and the angle until I feel that my current state of being is visible. That my current state of being is visible the way I want it. Stretching the aesthetic possibilities of who I think I am. Stretching the possibilities so that I fit in between.

It becomes more challenging to be who I thought I was. It becomes more complicated to look like who I am. The turns I twist myself into to stay who I was and the slide of who I will become. You don't have that problem. Not yet. I think. It remains guesswork.

How long will you outpace me? How quickly do I need to change to keep up with you? How centered should I position myself to lasso you? Because I will get you, that's for sure. I will do everything to achieve that. Delete.

Enough photos. I connect the camera to my laptop and start loading the pictures. I glance in the mirror again. I was bald between my twenties and thirties. I shaved it to setting two. I'll do that now too. Back then, I did it for intensity and practicality; now it's for clarity. Clippers. I start on the sides. From behind my ears to the front. It tickles. It feels refreshing. When I'm at the last and trickiest part, just below my crown, I see that it works. I still have a tight head. Not as aggressive as before, but certainly as effective. With a spinning motion, I run the clippers over my head a few more times. Remove the hard-to-reach long hairs just above my ears. There I stand. Almost naked. Perfect balance. Maybe I should join the Krishna or the military or go swimming. I love my own head.

You won't know what you're seeing when you encounter me. If I'm sexy with hair, try me without. Delete.

Enough bullshit. With a dustpan and brush, I sweep my excess hair off the floor and walk to the shower. Turn on the hot tap. All the mirrors in my house should fog up.

As thoughts swirl endlessly in my head, as if you were waving behind a glass wall, as if you were in a black hearse next to your bald, broad husband, shouting for him to step on the gas, as if you emerged from your house like a weatherman. Unpredictable. Is the sun shining, or is it raining? Delete.

Waking up while the day has already slipped away.

In the twilight zone where the sun is absent, and one night seamlessly transforms into another, with the life-giving source never gracing my skin, I wander through the deserted city. Thursday or something like that. The houses along the canal stand cluttered, their facades pressed against each other, as if invisible threads are holding them together in bundles, and the contents inside defiantly collide. Behind a few windows, light spills, and on closer inspection, I notice the beams lifting the ceilings with infinite patience. These houses were here before I existed. These structures, erected centuries ago solely for commodities, were built long before there was any inkling that I would tread here. Now, people inhabit these facades with open shutters. They have nothing to hide. Without curtains, the entire city can peer inside. They don't mind residing in a puppet show. On the contrary, they live where few others do, and only for that reason, they've taken on the thankless task of pretending as though claiming this for themselves is insignificant. I live like that too, only I became a bit paranoid from all those faces staring at me outside in the glow of the streetlights when I was just sitting on a chair reading a book. So, I hung up blinds. To protect myself and protect those people who find themselves overwhelmed by a guy who's adorned an ideal life for himself. From the outside. Admiration quickly slides into envy. The more seduction, the more the desire to lead someone else's life. Happiness is more fleeting than alcohol.

Above me, the sky has opened up. No moon tonight, only stars. I can't fathom all those beams of light that reach me after millions of light-years. I already find the ground beneath my feet distant. Sometimes, I get dizzy at the thought that the ground beneath my feet is never in the same spot in the universe at any given moment. Everything keeps spinning, everything changes, nothing remains as it was.

Perhaps death brings everything to a standstill. If I take the leap, I might be spat out into a motionless landscape, where everything was as it was, and nothing is susceptible to change anymore. Where was I before my birth? Or rather, before my conception? Or even earlier, before my mother was born, before life existed, before the big bang? Steps too large. Even if I could take such steps in my mind without realizing that life in general is utterly meaningless, even then, the thought alone is a hopelessly dead-end road. No one knows where we come from. No one knows where to. And as long as we try to figure out what lies beyond the boundaries of our existence, we will only be confronted with an order of emptiness. And if this life is nothing more than a cruel joke, why not enjoy the humorous ruthlessness with which this life has blessed me? Each moment, one by one. With the blinds down, my space is a cell with infinite dimensions. With my eyes closed, my head is a space with boundless possibilities. I can imagine anything, and undoubtedly, the possibility will arise to no longer die. Just like the former gods on Olympus had eternal life, I too will look around bored, seeking an adventure in which I will test the natural order, to see if there is a way out of hell.

The sun is shining, it's spring. The trees are filled with buds yet to bloom. The grass is still in hibernation. I am twelve. I cross the road. A car zooms by. Too fast. I can just jump aside, but feel the air vacuum on my skin. In less than a second, my life flashes before me. My brain works overtime to let all the images, feelings, thoughts pass by in less time than is possible. I stand trembling beside the road I just crossed, holding onto a tree. In the distance, I see the car vanish on the horizon. This is the movie everyone talks about. Does it only work when you're nearly dead? Does the movie always play? Or is there only a movie when it happens suddenly? The movie of your life as the last thing you experience. As an intense experience on the border from something to nothing. As the summary of everything you were.

As the key to something else

I have become accustomed to the pity that has been showered upon me from all sides. I even trust it. Everyone is constantly impressed by the living dead that I am. Especially because I look so good. It's incredible that beneath such a handsome guy, something is building up, gradually weakening him from the inside, so that he can suddenly die. I'm not sure how to interpret this attention, and since there seems to be no alternative, I just let it be. It happens in my blood. There, death is preparing itself. Very slowly and very efficiently. Elusive. As if nature has conspired against me. As if nature has decided that I'm not the center of creation. Foolish monkey. You never were. The more you scream that you're the center, the more you find yourself on the periphery. The more convinced you are of your own importance, the harder the elements will fight to prove that you are nothing. If you think your life has meaning, try dying. If only I could die. If only dying would come to an end. People around me drop dead as if it were nothing, while I keep on living. And if that makes me unhappy, then I'm doubly unfortunate. People die of old age, gently in their sleep. People die of cancer, due to an error in the duplication process. People get run over by trucks. People are shot dead, accidentally or intentionally. People jump from tall buildings, in front of trains, off high bridges. People hang themselves, in the garage, in the attic, or in a dark room. People are torn to pieces or cut themselves, preferably in the bath. Some hearts fail, and people collapse on the street, in a restaurant, or while showering. People walk into the water with stones in their pockets or go swimming after taking a tube of sleeping pills or fall into a ditch on something hallucinogenic. Trains collide. Cars crash into each other. Air pressure drops, and everyone freezes. Helicopters crash. People don't make it out of their burning house. In a senior citizens' flat, a little old lady falls against the heater and is found skinned. In the ravine lies the adulterous husband. On the beach, a child's body washes ashore. A few young men blow themselves up and unsuspecting bystanders. Visitors are gassed by the government. The parachute doesn't open. The machines are shut down. During a commercial flight over the Pacific Ocean, a piece falls out of the fuselage at ten kilometers altitude. Someone stares for minutes at the cool waters of their death.

The black leather three-seater doesn't sleep well. The armrests are just too high, and the surface I lie on is just too short. So, I keep waking up with a stiff neck or numb legs. Walking is no longer an option, just like eating. I only get a plate of soup, a piece of bread, or maybe a small package of yogurt down my throat. If I need to go to the bathroom, it takes forever. I run out of breath. If Tiger isn't around, I crawl on the floor to the threshold that leads me into the hallway. Once in the hallway, I crawl over the threshold that leads me to the toilet. Now just five meters on hands and knees, and with tremendous effort, I get myself onto the toilet. Dazed, I stay there. I never know how long. Time is a vast territory between waking up. When Tiger comes home or leaves, he lets me sleep. Tiger works. Five days a week. He's gone every morning at half-past seven. Home every evening at six. Friends come by a few times a week. Shocked and full of attention. It's not going well. I'm glad they visit. We play music, watch a movie, or just chat. After those visits, I'm dead. *There she is. Like an innocently smiling girl, she lies against me. She means no harm. She's happy that she can reassure me. With big eyes, she looks at me. I don't have to be afraid, she says. Everything will be fine. No past. No future. Only now, and now is good. A fresh alpine meadow where a thousand flowers bloom. A sunny autumn day where the strands of mist disappear on their own. A cool summer evening in which the full moon makes you feel like a day that will never end. A quiet winter morning with snowflakes gently falling on black branches. A fluffy little fox with big ears exploring the world and frolicking after a butterfly. Tender green grass. The smell of wet pavement when the hot day gives way to a thunderstorm.*

I know the room where I lie like the back of my hand. Four thick walls and a high ceiling. On the black linoleum lies a blood-red carpet with cheerfully dancing folkloric nomads. All simple. The sofa is in a corner between two windows. One window provides a view between the houses, more houses, branches of trees. The other window looks out onto a blind wall. Behind the sofa is a white glass half-egg on two slender, tall, black metal pipes. In front of the window with a view is a huge ficus plant. In the ceiling above me, there is a crack. From one window to the other, almost an equilateral triangle, except that one of the lines is slightly curved. As if the walls merging into the ceiling form the thread of a simple arc where an invisible arrow is strung. When I painted the ceiling, I filled the crack with putty, but it didn't help. The crack came back, and now it laughs at me through the latex, grinning at me from the ceiling, unable to help itself. *There she is. Like a seductive old whore, she lies against me. She means no harm. She's happy that she can reassure me. With heavily made-up eyes, she looks at me. I don't have to be afraid, she says. Everything will be fine. The past. The future. Everything is okay. A wild overgrown heath where a herd of sheep wanders. Mist spreading between the trees. A dark winter afternoon where the water streaking against the window freezes before it reaches the windowsill. A bird of prey circling above the field. A fox hiding in the underbrush, waiting for the bloodhounds that will find him howling.*

Numb, slowly torn to shreds, bit by bit, I disappear cautiously. As if my body understands itself and rounds off everything I've ever experienced in my brain. Stupefied, I sit there smiling in the black glossy three-seater. I need nothing more, nothing is more important, everything is good, there's nothing more that wants to come to mind, there's nothing more I need to say, nothing more to think. *There she is. Like a sneaky thief, she comes to rob me. She means no harm. She's sorry she can't reassure me. Black, almost invisible, I feel the gleam of her eyes shooting past me. There's nothing to be done. I can worry, but it's unnecessary. She's just doing her job. She does her job well. She does it in such a way that I barely notice. A shadow in the clouds among the bushes. A leaf falling prematurely from a tree. A moonless night turning into a sunless day. A fish darting under the ice. A motionless heron. The smell of chlorine in a public swimming pool.*

"Shall I take you to the emergency room?" Tiger asks. Knives open my body. I cough my lungs out. "I'll get the car."

Needles in my arms. An oxygen mask on my head. A cold plate for X-rays. Rolled into a dark room.

Nurses come to see me and chat. Tiger is there. Every day. With books, food, music. A doctor who is also a professor shows me to about fifty students. The light in the lecture hall blinds me. Fruit and magazines.

Peter comes to cut my hair. A camouflage pajama. Me in a wheelchair. Stephan in a cow costume. Brass band playing a few classics outside my window on Sunday morning. A man with whom I share the room. Spanish. Not dead yet. Not yet.

Ten days later

Pumped with life, I find myself back on the glossy black three-seater. It wasn't my time yet, says Tiger.

The nightclub slowly fills with silent people. A flowing melody with soft drums drifts casually through the high baroque space. The curtains on the stage are closed, the bar is open, and everyone is drinking champagne. When the hall is full, the music stops. The lights in the hall go out, a spotlight moves to the center of the curtains, which open with a graceful motion. On an empty stage hangs a bright red, sequin-decorated, torn, tiny dress on a thread. Slowly, a wild mass of black hair descends until it hangs above the dress. The music starts. A mournful rock song about a woman who can't handle it all. How fitting, I think, and smile. Meanwhile, I continue living and wonder what I did to deserve this. The pills I take make the world stand at a distance, as if I'm staring through a reversed telescope. I gain ten kilos within a week, and my skin begins to crack. I have to go to the bathroom at the most inconvenient times, which I often don't make, so I always carry a clean pair of underwear in my coat pocket. The attention fades, there's no more glory to be had, yet I continue living, right? Stop whining. Now! I keep my mouth shut and no longer understand what life is. How many years have I missed? Five? Six? Seven?

Together with my mother, I sit under the chandeliers in a grand café. Everyone knows by now that I don't have much time left, except her. How do you tell your mother that you're dying? She's dressed in her best clothes with her hair curled. There you go. I couldn't manage it when I was at her farm, and I really couldn't get that letter out of my pen, so tell her now. She reacts matter-of-factly. Does it have something to do with Italy? she asks. I don't know. She sighs.

Just like your father

In the meantime, I realize that I'm alive between activities, but whether it makes sense, I don't know. Must life have meaning? Is it necessary to live with an idea in mind so that, once the end has come, you can close your eyes, and everyone can complain to their heart's content that they miss you so much? I don't know, and I decide to stop taking my pills. A cowardly way to commit suicide, if you want to see it that way, but this is the best option at the moment. Besides, shouldn't I always give myself the chance to reconsider my choices? A bit awkward if I end up as a pile of blood and bones on the sidewalk of that tall building. A bit messy if I lie on the ground with a hole in my head. A bit careless if I dangle from the rafters. A bit tragic if I'm scraped off the nose of a train. A slow suicide, if such a thing exists, is allowed for me. I found it inconvenient to take my pills at two different times every day anyway. My doctor approves; there are others who take a vacation. I mainly want to test if I still want to live. The months pass with boring regularity. There are weeks when I don't see anyone. Stupidly, I wait for the end in my own death cell.

Optimism rarely lasts more than a month, and knowing this, I try to do as much as possible. So much that, when the ink-black clouds come drifting in again, I lie feverish in my bed. These are the times that don't understand me. They don't let me sleep, and when I finally fall asleep with the wish never to wake up again, I sleep more intensely and longer than I can justify. The black clouds become darker and more powerful. My desire for death becomes more logical, more obvious. Even misery has its limits. I imagine what it's like not to be there anymore. Not having to wake up anymore. Not having to be. Not having to think. Never having to look at myself in the mirror again. Actually, I'm already not here. I don't open the door anymore, I don't answer the phone anymore, I don't react when someone speaks to me. I sit in my room, and everything is too much for me. I can't watch TV, I can't hear music, I can't read words. All I can do is lie in the dark with my eyes closed in my bed. I don't want to feel anything, think anything, be anything. Apathetic. Just lying flat on my back. But every now and then, I have to get up to get something to drink or to go to the bathroom. That's the least I do. And if I have a revival and start feeling hungry, I toss and turn endlessly in my bed. Then, I reluctantly turn on the TV. Then, I reluctantly put on my clothes. Then, I reluctantly go to the snackbar for a gyro fries. Life has won again.

We are selfish animals. We know what we can

perceive, and after that, it's guesswork, fantasy, hypotheses. Usually, we wish our dead the afterlife they believe in, but no one has come back from the underworld to tell us what it's like there.

There's a knock on my door; I'm sleeping. There's another knock, I wake up. Is someone at my door? Half crumpled, I step out of my bed, which I call the carriage, and, dizzy, I walk to the door. It's ice-cold; I have no heating in my bedroom, just an electric blanket, and I sleep naked. I pull down the handle and open the door. It's my father. I let him in and quickly lie back in my bed with my blankets over me. My father looks for a spot on my clothes that I've thrown messily on a rickety rattan chair. So, I lie in my bed, looking at my father. He looks different. He's young again. Black wavy hair, deep dark eyes under black bushy eyebrows, a straight nose, small ears. Without effort, he rolls a cigarette. He lights it and, unhindered by the cold, smokes. Leaving rings of smoke in the frozen air of my room. Reassured, I fall asleep. The next morning, he's gone, along with the smoke.

Thursday, May 11, evening

I need to eat. I forgot to go to the supermarket, and they're already closed. I'll get pizza or something Eastern. At the intersection, there's a Japanese, a Javanese, a Chinese, a Thai. An Asian intersection. It's a good neighborhood. I don't know what I feel like. I'll just walk and see what I end up bringing home.

I can't decide. But I also have to eat. The Chinese place is always nice. Good takeout and a cool woman who can take orders over the phone with an earpiece while overseeing everything in her shop. A family business. Brothers, husband, and mother in the kitchen. Children flutter in and out. Keeping the waiting customers entertained with chatter. The cool woman recognizes me even when I don't enter her store. She's waving amidst all the hustle and bustle. I'm not really hungry. I order a spring roll and the Chinese hors d'oeuvre, a mix of fried balls with sweet and sour sauce, and prawn crackers. I sit down on a green chair covered with vinyl. My grandma also had such chairs. And peanut brittle and raspberry lemonade and comic books and fifty other grandchildren. No wonder she lost track sometimes.

Damn, it's already nine o'clock. I finished my meal and am sitting at the yellow table with the mint-green base. There's really nothing I can do today. Should I roll a joint? I've already smoked almost two packs of Marlboro. Easy now. I stand up. Grab the plastic containers that held my dinner and expertly squish them together. Put them in the plastic bag my food was delivered in. I throw the bag in the trash, an old metal bucket that was probably a trash can even before. I found it on the street once. The year

1962 on the lid and a number: 558939.
Whatever that means.

Here you are. You probably already know; you are the center of this world. Nothing happens here without your consent. Nothing has value unless you've given it value. Things only have names after you've visited. That's how important you are. The only one aware of your own existence. The only one who can give it meaning. The only one who knows if it's worthwhile. Death, you can always do that. It will surely happen. Until then, you're in charge. You're a free person with unlimited possibilities. Enjoy it. You're a freak of nature, like everything around you. Nature organizes. Everything. How much food there is, how much drink. Who survives, who dies. Who has power, who doesn't. Who's rich, who isn't. So you live for centuries on end. Of course, you complain about others who make your life miserable, about yourself, that you're so ignorant. But that doesn't stop you from living. From hating, loving. You're the end result of millions of years of organization, chance, capriciousness. A logical consequence of unpredictability. Leaving and will leave traces. Don't have illusions. Nature isn't perfect and precise; that's what makes it complete. As a result of so much chance, let's say, as the end station of all that time between the beginning and now, you're the only thing that still matters. It lives in your head. Like a thunderstorm, your brain rages. To understand all those useful and interesting things around you that don't have names yet. You're eager to dive into it. To sort it. To label it. To carefully pack it into boxes, which you seal with the thickest tape you can find and stack them where you store your boxes, somewhere in your head. That's you. It's in you. Everything has its place.

Hastily, you go through your life. You want to be everywhere. Miss nothing, and certainly not be the last one to find out something. Knowledge is power. Degenenerate. If you had to do it all over again, you'd choose the same path. As if chance doesn't exist. As if you've chosen this life yourself. As if no one will call you to account for what you've done with your life. Only you know if it's worth it. Only you know if you have meaning.

The record gets stuck again.

I spend a whole Saturday afternoon in a space— correction: The Space, to learn to meditate. Fourteen women, men are always in the minority in these courses. The course leader is named Karl. He's an economist. After a severe RSI attack that lasted a year and a half, he started meditating. No spiritual stuff here. Just essence. We quickly learn the body scan, breathing, and mantra meditation. In between, Karl tells us more about meditating and why it's so good. I'm going to do this for the rest of my life. If only to get rid of you. Delete.

I have to impose rules on myself. Boundaries I must not cross. Like not sending you messages randomly. That privilege is now in your corner. I was starting to feel like a stalker. I was about to check the back of your house to see what Bas's last name was. But I changed my mind at the last moment. I stood with my bike on the corner and didn't pass by your front door. Not a good idea to know who Bas is. I shouldn't get involved. You mentioned that he was broad and bald. And that he was beaten up by your dealer during your vacation in Tuscany. God knows why.

Yet, I came across the sales page of your house on the internet. I suspect that Bas bought your house before he met you. He paid 234,000 euros for it. The house. On the real estate agent's site, I could freely view your living room, kitchen, bedroom, and balcony. Nice of them. Now I know where you spend your life. I don't care. I think. But, of course, I've already gone too far. Delete.

I have to stop this. Even if you confess that you desperately want to be with me. Delete.

I act tough as if everything is fine. As if it's not a problem that you're not next to me every day when I fall asleep. As if it's not a problem to wake up every day without you beside me. As if it's not a problem that I don't smell you daily. Delete.

It doesn't matter what I do or say. I'm like a man without arms. Like a mindless animal sitting in an expansive empty space. Eyes like saucers. Ears flat on my head. The faster everything is over, the longer I can enjoy it. I push myself back into my chair. Jump off the platform. Stuff another pill in. Forget everything. In a room with a screen, I press a button. I'm somewhere else. I press that button, and I think I know. I press that button, and I forget.

Can you control yourself? Your thoughts like a joystick. Your emotions sharper. Your body harder. How it felt to be in love. How it is to stand on a deserted beach. The longer you can hold onto that thought, the longer happiness whispers by your head. You can love yourself by looking in the mirror. You're dependent. On the opinions of others. Avoiding pain. Setting aside desires.

Deep within me, it seems to me that I'm deceiving you. Strange. As if you could sense what's going on with me. Like I wonder about all those small, seemingly insignificant feelings I keep having, coming out of nowhere, and then suddenly there's an email from you. Or you call. Or you don't call, but later you say you wanted to call me. Or you open an email from me and get upset. Or you get the flu, and the right side of my face goes numb. Or you have an ear infection, and there's a constant ringing and buzzing in my right ear. Even when you want to see me but forbid yourself. I feel that too. It's very tricky. These illusions. Because I know they can't be true. They can't be explained, right? Just like it's inexplicable why two people fall in love. Or one in the other. Or me in you. Why now. Delete.

Delete. Delete. Delete. Delete. Delete. Delete.
Delete. Delete. Delete. Delete. Delete. Delete.
Delete. Delete. Delete. Delete. Delete. Delete.
Delete. Delete. Delete. Delete. Delete. Delete.
Delete. Delete. Delete. Delete. Delete. Delete.
Delete. Delete. Delete. Delete. Delete. Delete.
Delete. Delete. Delete. Delete. Delete. Delete.
Delete. Delete. Delete. Delete. Delete. Delete.
Delete. Delete. Delete. Delete. Delete. Delete.
Delete. Delete. Delete.

Nobody knows less, nobody knows better, nobody knows anything, nobody knows everything. I've had to think long about my role. Who I am doesn't matter, only my role. Letting go of the ego is using the ego. Like a mirror. What you see is yourself. Seeing and being seen. I know who I am. I know where I'm going. I know what my life is about. I can do something other than just thinking. Stop sitting in my head all the time. Damn it, look around. Feel where I am. Know who I am. Do what I feel like doing, for once be myself. And stop thinking. In the silence where my brain is nothing more than a reflection of what's happening around me, I see a lone skater glide over a white landscape on a canal. That skater is me. The ice is of the best quality, smooth with few air bubbles between the thin air and the black water. My rhythm is almost perfect. Tsjak-tsj, tsjak-tsj, tsjak-tsj. Skating straight, back straight, bend my knees, hips back, switch, push off with the middle of my foot, hands loosely resting on my buttocks, nose in the wind, sunglasses. Behind the reeds, endless meadows, occasional clumps of trees, and in the distance, between some scattered trees, the white roof of a farmhouse. The perfect nothing. Just me, my rhythm, and the ice propelling me towards a point on the horizon where the white curve turns into an intense blue pressed tight against the sky. A white-yellow ball spews a sharp dark shadow in the top right, cold air turns into steam as it escapes my body again, my heart beats to the rhythm of hypnosis. In my ear, eternity rushes by. Reality feels different than I think it should. Why I set such demands for myself, I don't know. I don't like being fooled. I don't like breathing in polluted air. I hate it when the sounds reaching my ears deceive me. I detest it when the images I see are meant to frighten me, alienate me, flatten me. I'm disgusted by scents that are fake, that pretend to be real but only serve to rob all the life inside me of its erection. I dream of being touched. By something or someone or nothing. Butterflies circling around my head. Birds tapping on my window. Cows stepping through the world in amazement. I try to concentrate. The birches next to my house, the shadow of the sun in the valley, the insects swarming above the grass, the slight friction of the rope my hammock slides along the wood, the scent of mountain air, the color of my skin, and how the hairs on my legs seem to be silver-blond in the grazing light. I'll probably always recognize my own face, no matter how much the cartilage in my ears and nose expands, no matter how much gravity stretches my skin, no matter how big the pores on my cheeks become. I had those eyes in the womb; I'll keep having them until I die. Maybe they'll wear out a bit, maybe they'll have seen a bit too much, maybe they'll see less and less, they'll remain those same marbles they were when I was two, or eighteen, or thirty-two. What I achieve is clear. I've forgotten the expectations I had when I grew up. Days come, days go. And I do my thing as well as I can. Yet, I suspect that there is more, that there is more than just, that there is the possibility, if only to. From my unique position, conquered by myself. My own life. That of others. Overview. I wonder what. I can oversee. The world. Is big. There are many others. More and more, it seems. Everyone wants a piece. The place underneath. Own time to do what. The world turning. Building in happiness. Generating energy. Accumulated anger. Strange rule of my kind. Amazed, defeating, surprising. So far it has come. The reasons for this history are. The unlikely victory. Primate. Folly of an animal that forgets its roots. Unfortunate coincidence of circumstances. Right to its own existence. Carelessness with which.

Does it claim that right?

Sometimes I'm in my house, and I feel like someone is staring at me. I look up, but there's no one. Does something need a body to observe me? Which force is stronger? Present looks into the future. The future examines the past. The more I know, the more questions. The list will always keep growing. Often, only the questions are enough. I don't need to know everything. Knowledge is more. A form of less. The more I know. The better. I know there are no. Fixed answers. A form of freedom. A form of certainty. I know who I am and what I can. The limits of my existence. Clear. I can't bypass them. To be able to be who I am. Think who I am. What others think who I could be. Nothing is truly impossible. If I think about it. Reality is liquid. If I imagine. Freedom a form of certainty. Those feelings I had no idea existed. By now, I'm accomplished. I thought. Until I met you.

Abyss.

III SHADOWLAND

I cycle on my new bike. On my way to acupuncture. One of the nine streets. The sun is shining directly in my face. A pigeon sits on the street. Pigeons usually fly away when you approach them with your bike. Not this one. It stays put. In the doorway of the coffee shop, a boy watches it happen. I cycle over the pigeon. Curse. As hard as I can. See my thin tire break a spine. Stop. Walk back. Ask the boy, who has entered the coffee shop completely bewildered and is now back outside, what to do. The pigeon flutters onto the sidewalk with one wing. Pathetic. Hit by a bike. By me. Fuck. 'Animal ambulance,' says the coffee shop boy. I know the pigeon is beyond saving. It's still alive now, but it'll be dead by tonight. I heard a crack. Its little spine. The animal ambulance costs money. A lot of money. I'm broke. Completely bewildered. Decide to keep cycling. Life is life. Why did the pigeon stay? Was it confused by the smell of the coffee shop? Am I cycling so fast that the pigeons can't gauge it anymore? Was it an old pigeon with so many ailments that it couldn't fly anymore? Was the pigeon depressed and on a suicide mission? Can pigeons be depressed? Do pigeons commit suicide?

Most delicious on earth

It's Friday. Today would have been a day when I held you in my arms. And be very close to you. I would whisper sweet words in your ear. Tell you all my secrets. We would just be normal lovers. You wouldn't be confused because you trusted your heart instead of your head. But today is not like that. You'll be at home, waking up, maybe still a bit under the weather, but not as bad as yesterday or the day before. You'll lie in the garden because the weather is so beautiful and make some calls to friends. Your husband will come home from work and make an extra effort to please you because it sucks that you have the flu. I can't imagine how you are with your husband. I can have all kinds of fantasies, but it doesn't change my situation. I'm empty-handed. Illusion. A life that belongs only to me. Forced. Because you're not here. How on earth can I show you that I miss you, that I long for you, that all I want is you?

Of course, I think of you. I'm sentimental enough. But I don't really miss you. I hope. I constantly wonder what it was that made us run towards each other and what it was that made you turn around immediately when I got too close. What happened? How did I come across? What did you really want? Or was it truly a blinded moment that's difficult to trace afterward? If I weren't with Bas, I would have been with you long ago. You say it. I listen. Can't believe it, but I have to. On the screen, people from the distant future pass by, as envisioned forty years ago. If I weren't with Bas, I would have been with you long ago. I let these words circle through my mind. I taste them. Syllable after syllable. You hang next to me on a bench in the dark. You hold my hand. You don't want to let me go. You can't let me go. I see you shoot past when I enter. You see me, crouch, and sneak past me as fast as you can. I find it amusing. My face still isn't okay. I know which expression works best. The one without. Don't smile. I know where you are. All the time. You're talking on the dance floor. Pretending to have a good time. I can do that too. Even better. Vincent is getting drunk. I'm just drinking coke. I want to experience this. Completely. If I weren't with Bas, I would have been with you long ago. I join a group of cool people. They're clearly messed up. Sweating and moving with grotesque out-of-time movements. I laugh and dance with them. Meanwhile, I keep an eye on you. I see you talking to the guy you always use as an excuse to see me. If I weren't with Bas, I would have been with you long ago. I tell you that there's nothing I want more than you. You want nothing more than me.

If I weren't with Bas, I would have been with you long ago. This Bas must be very special. I don't know him. Don't even know if I want to know him. I respect him. He's had you for three years. How did he manage that? I envy him like very few people can envy someone. You really belong to me. In my thoughts, there's a long line of certainty that you will be mine someday. If I weren't with Bas, I would have been with you long ago. 'Come on, let's go,' I say. You look at me sheepishly. I say I'm going home and you're going to keep dancing. I need to express myself better. If I weren't with Bas, I would have been with you long ago. Finally, you have the courage to send an email announcing that it will be your last. We know that. Nothing is the last for us. We will always continue. No matter when and how. We could do this a million more times, like being born when we die. I'm fine with that. If I weren't with Bas, I would have been with you long ago. As long as it eventually happens. Now would be a good time. Now lasts basically forever. You write that you don't feel butterflies anymore. I believe you. I don't feel butterflies either. What I feel is more of a caked-up lie that I—no matter how I struggle—have to believe. You write that you're sure you've hurt me a lot. If only you knew what pain was. If only you knew who I was. Just as I can't get a grip on you, you will never get a grip on me. All your thoughts about me can go straight into the shredder because you have no idea who you're dealing with. Thankfully. Fortunately, you can't imagine what I feel and what I must feel. Sometimes I think I called you upon me as a punishment. To renew my karma. Or something like that. To come to terms with my own stupid behavior. For example. You think you're bad. You think you've hurt me. Think again. My messages, which initially charmed you, you now call 'disturbing'. Crushing. If I weren't with Bas, I would have been with you long ago. Pain is nothing more than a way to gain insight. You don't hurt me. Pain is something I generate myself, just like I generated my love for you, just like I could see myself in you. Like you think you can see yourself in me. How are you really doing now? I'm fine, thank you. How are you really doing now? Do you really think you can look me in the eyes now? Do you really think you can just continue with what you were doing? Do you really think I'll swoon if you show me your dick? How are you really doing now? From a distance, you watch me. You think you have me under control, but you have no control. Not over Bas, not over yourself, not over me. You think you can get away with everything. Good luck. How are you really doing now? How are you really doing now? How are you really doing now? I'm doing well. My face is back, and my heart still beats where it always has. My head is still as tangled as ever. Thankfully, otherwise I couldn't handle it. I need to wake up, I think. I need to be normal. For whom, actually? How are you really doing now? But what I keep forgetting is that I'm only truly awake when I'm with you. How are you really doing now? How would I be doing? What do you think? Yes, I'm annoyed that I never wake up next to you. Yes, I'm upset about how things went down. If I weren't with Bas, I would have been with you.

How are you really doing now? Come, dance with me. Come, let's take a photo. Come, hang out on the couch with me. You smell amazing. How are you really doing now? Your mother thinks you could start studying again. I say, 'Do it, what do you want to study?' 'Art Academy,' you say. Why not? You don't know how to finance it. Your mother can pay for it if she thinks it's such a good plan. She says, 'Bas would probably be willing to help.' If I weren't with Bas, I would have been with you long ago. I see on your site that Bas has taken over the business management of your theater group. Cool of him. He must be a man without real problems. Someone who sails through life easily and has you as a playmate, while you control his decisions behind the scenes. Extort his confidence. Demand a roof over your head. Shape your life the way you want. If you weren't with Bas, you would have been with me long ago. You know what? I believe you. But if you really felt something for me, you would have been with me long ago. If you really followed your heart, we would see each other every morning now. If you really followed your heart, there would be no need for acting. Everything would be real, and no day would be the same. How am I really doing now? I'll tell you. It sucks.

Micha is cool. He's from Dresden, and I'll meet him in the darkroom of a disco where too many naked bodies dance too blatantly to loud music with too much rhythm. First, he'll kiss me in the corridor, and when we both have a hard-on, he'll suggest going into a booth where the cheapest porn on a small screen sets the mood. I'll fuck him, and it'll be so good that when we later share a coke, exhausted, on a bench, I'll invite myself to go to his place, where he'll then fuck me on his loft bed while I try to find support with my feet against the ceiling. He'll sigh that it's been a long time since he fucked someone, and I'll just say sweet things, for example, about his nose, which has such a beautiful blunt shape, and where the hairs of his eyebrows are making a very gentle start. He'll tell me about a metro station in Moscow with chandeliers, where he waited for a connection to the airport the day before. And he'll also say that next weekend he's going to an island in the Wadden Sea to celebrate the twenty-year anniversary of his ex's parents' marriage. He's not looking forward to it. His own parents will be there too. He works, like you, in a hospital. In the leukemia ward. Ideally, he would like to delve into aeronautical engineering, and he has a site with photos he took of his friends. The next morning, it will be gray in Berlin. It will rain all day. Micha has to work at one. At twelve, we'll climax one last time. Then we'll both take a shower and the S-Bahn. I'll introduce you to Micha when he's here or if we ever hang out together in Berlin. Micha is nice.

Friday, June 9

Boldly forward

Dearest Tiger,

I also enjoyed having you here. Funny that you managed to get hold of that GHB. Did it make its way to Kloten disguised as Evian?

Thank you for your concise feedback. I hope I can maintain the momentum.

Today is a free day, and it's time to tackle my administration. I hate it so much. But before the creditors come knocking on my door, I'll have to make sure to get back in financial balance. Why do I have such an aversion to understanding money?

Last weekend, I was in Berlin, and I have to tell you that I rarely feel as at home as there. I was full of melancholy in the S-Bahn. I so did not want to go back to fairytale village Amsterdam, and just wanted to stay and stay. Now, I must mention that the weather was good, and everyone was in good spirits. Maybe I should spend a summer there after all. Even if it's just for the one-euro döner kebab.

Everything is going well in fairytale village. I'm writing. Maurice is in Italy with his husband, but before they left, we promised each other to become friends. Of course, I'm still just as confused about the matter as before. My face is doing well; acupuncture is the solution, so if you ever come across someone with Bell's palsy... The needles go in again this afternoon. At four.

Is everything going well in Züri? Is everyone already in the lake there? On Monday, I'm cycling on my brand new bike to Zandvoort for a day of sun and sports. In the evening, there's a barbecue planned in Vondelpark. Ah, idyll! !

Much love to Tristan and a big KISS from the old wolf to yourself.

I just had my final acupuncture treatment from Chi Fung Lee, the Hong Kong Chinese, who keeps telling me how important it is to drink plenty of water and soy milk, especially when I lose myself in alcohol, which isn't that often. Today he talks about the benefits of spirulina. I have to take good care of my body. The paralysis is caused by an overloaded liver, low resistance, and too much stress. I also have to make sure not to expose myself to the wind too much when I've been drinking. That's very dangerous.

Friday, July 7

Sommer in the City!

Hey, dearest Tiger,

That sounds delicious! Give my regards to everyone in the villa.

The summer is pretty good here, although it was very humid last week, making it quite muggy. I was sitting topless at the office and didn't feel very productive. Of course, that turned out to be relative.

My face is back to normal (all wrinkles are back), and I'm writing a piece for the next newsletter about the benefits of acupuncture. Following Mr. Chi Fung Lee's advice, who has treated me so carefully and excellently, I now drink a glass of soy milk every day. After the meditation course, I spend fifteen minutes every day being still, focusing on my breathing, chanting mantras, or tensing and relaxing different parts of my body. I highly recommend all of this to you.

In love, I'm less fortunate. Maurice is still on my mind all the time. I've now decided to be a bit less assertive with this love and see what happens if I let him take the lead. However, I'm increasingly skeptical that it will 'turn out well' in the sense of hooray, we're so happy together! It causes more pain than pleasure, although the joy that arises after some contact, either physical or in writing, albeit short-lived, is somewhat ecstatic. I'll probably miss that.

I did meet an incredibly nice guy when I was in Berlin a month ago. His name is Micha, and our contact is starting to take on the contours of a cautious romance, especially now that my bosses have asked me to accompany them to a conference in Leipzig at the end of August. This conference seems to be crucial for the agency, and I've enthusiastically signed up for workshops on drugs and relationships.

But Micha is very attractive and fun, and I'm quite confused because, of course, I don't really want to say goodbye to my 'difficult love.' I'll probably have to make a choice before Micha shows up at my doorstep in three weeks.

So, the life of the old Wolf is good. The only objection is called Maurice, but he's currently spending a weekend in Milan, shaking hands with Bas's future employees as a respectable husband. This Bas, my unwelcome rival who doesn't even know of my existence, is becoming the director of something there.

Lots of love from today's somewhat cloudy but not unpleasant Amsterdam. Give Tristan the warmest greetings from me.

Kisses from the old Wolf

Micha is sweet. And delicious. He arrived at nine in the evening. We didn't need much time to get used to each other, as we were already talking every day between four and six hours on Skype. I had cleaned my house. With dynamite. That's how it looks. Spotless. Eric had given me a bottle of a miracle substance from an Antillean pharmacy. Amor Amor. "You have to believe in it," he added. Either put your loved one in a bath with this stuff or clean your house with it. I don't have a bath, so it was the floor. On my knees, I thoroughly scrubbed every corner with the stuff. Just before Micha arrived, I also scattered some drops of the substance here and there. Just to be sure. It didn't help.

I told him about you. Being honest. How you bother me. And how you don't reject me. Being honest. And how much you want to be with me. And how impossible this is. Being honest. How your problem is mine.

I run into you on the canal, and you shout after me, "I'll email you!" You don't email me.

I see you in the Unk, and you say, "Friday at eleven?" But you're not there on Friday at eleven. You'll contact me, you say. But I hear nothing from you.

I see you on the street. You're drinking. You see me and startle. I see the shock on your face. It's everywhere. You're afraid. I've become a threat. I don't know what for.

Micha keeps saying that I should come over, but when I try to make plans, he becomes anxious. For himself, he says. I don't know what to think. Just stay in Amsterdam. I've given him many compliments. He evokes them in me as I evoke them in others. Both of us don't fit into our bodies. It's too clear, too beautiful; it raises too many questions. We don't trust ourselves to be ourselves. Why do you want me then? What is so special about me that you want me? You know it's an impossible situation, right? We will never meet. We will never be able to look each other in the eyes, if only because we can't see anything else but what we ourselves are. And then everything just continues. I'll keep doing my thing, and you'll do yours.

Wednesday, August 9

Re: New York / Maderanertal

Tiger!

Yes, very curious about the new kitchen! When should I come to inspect it? Should I just buy a ticket to Zurich when I have the money? I'll call you about that.

What a delightful life you have! New York is amazing, right? I assume you didn't venture far from Manhattan? Or were there business matters in the Bronx and Brooklyn? I read in the newspaper here that the sparrows were falling from the rooftops. Were you there during that hot period? The only two times I was in New York, it was either very hot or very cold. I'm very curious about how it is there in spring or autumn. Does Tristan have many friends there? Nice to immediately be in nature. I miss the mountains.

Micha was here last week, and I had actually planned to be in Berlin now, but that turns out not to be the case. I have two weeks off from the office, and I wanted to enjoy them with Micha. He's really a great guy. But every time it came up to come to Berlin, he was first very enthusiastic, and then, as the thought sank in, suddenly very thoughtful. When the reaction was still so thoughtful after the fourth time, I started thinking differently about him, which is a shame. It was very nice to have him here. We had a lot of sex and smoked a lot, and we also had some fun discussions, but the spark that was there during our email exchange and the many hours on Skype was somewhat missing. I don't know exactly why. He was a bit passive, and I didn't feel like taking the lead all the time. Of course, there was also the issue that I rushed toward him to get away from the other one. In my thoughts.

That didn't really work. I've run into the other one a few times now, and I don't know if I find it enjoyable to constantly witness that shocked reaction on the face I fantasized so much about a few months ago. I try to avoid him as much as possible, but Amsterdam is small, and you can't turn your ass without bumping into each other. Then I just nod politely, but internally, it burns.

This past Monday, I thought of throwing myself to the lions again. The Same Place is a spot where you can mess around with FKK on Monday evenings. I've been going to the gym a lot these days, and in the semi-darkness, I must look imposing because every time I stood in a quiet spot, it quickly became crowded. Then I just let everyone in until I'd had enough and pushed those hungry old men away again. It didn't make me happy. When I thought to check out the darkroom of the Eagle at around two in the morning, a handsome Canadian followed me. He had Brad Pitt eyes and couldn't have been older than thirty. But I had to admit that I couldn't handle it at that moment, and after one beer, I just walked home.

My luck is not currently with men. I'm thinking about how I want to do the coming months and am beginning to realize that a lot of work is ahead. The past few days, I've been almost continuously writing, and although it might all be a bit too fresh, I'm starting to understand what has happened to me in the past half year. And because he was a man with passion, the sun shone. I'll send you the story. Still need to process it and such. But then you'll understand a bit how things are. It's like I have to try some different paths. Or just focus less on love.

Also, alter Tiger!

No parade for a while? If I had to choose between music on wheels in my own city and fireworks over Lake Geneva, I would also know what to pick! Enjoy it. Say hi to Tristan and everyone else you talk to.

Love from the old Wolf

Shadowland

Likely a regular Thursday evening. Time flowed effortlessly, the street filled with various characters, and he was amidst them. He thought of you, and because he was a man of passion, the sun was shining. It was that incredibly long summer. The summer that lingered. Everyone anticipated autumn and felt guilty for not appreciating a summer you didn't need a plane for. Nothing else happened. The sun hung in a cloudless sky, warmth enveloped the city, and later, the street transformed into an endless barbecue with guitars playing in the background.

Like anyone who had converted air into matter, he knew that the real art was to give back that same matter to the air. Nothing more, nothing less. That's why he had only himself left.

He was content with himself. He was happy to be able to be himself without all the baggage weighing him down. Dragging him off balance. Inflating him to outrageous proportions. Making him stumble so that he'd shatter into a thousand pieces. He had managed to sidestep that danger. He had managed to shake off his ego, which clung to him like a dark shadow. He had managed to be free of himself. And now, he only thought of you.

How empty a full life can be, that full his was. He looked around and felt how the street undulated in a lazy happiness. In the sunglasses around him, a relaxed orange glow reflected, rendering all the harsh questions of life unnecessary. On the corner of the street, five boys sat on a blanket, chanting mantras in a language that came from afar and above to give balance to the dizzying valley of the wayward city. Today, that balance had tilted towards all the good he could imagine. Everything was fine. Purified, pure, he felt like an installation that filtered out polluted air, an energy field where only love could survive.

In the multitude of reflections in the small square windows, collectively forming a large window, our man vaguely saw himself. Behind him, it seemed as if the world had expanded, shot out, transformed into a mass of hot air and light. The man pondered how he would find you through all those reflections. He knew how to turn nothing into something and how to turn something into nothing, but in his vacuum-like self, he hadn't found a solution to connect, maybe even blend, with another; with you. He didn't even know where to find you, let alone how to reach you and, once he found you, how to address you. Only when he would meet you, and that would be at a moment when you least expected it— it always was—, it would be revealed that you couldn't pronounce each other's names without practicing a lot. Vowels and consonants had to be pronounced separately. Slowly at first, as in a game, and then faster and faster, so that the impossible names could breeze through, reaching your hearts, making you feel like you were never alone again. And you would believe it, just like him, because he wouldn't lose himself in his secrets and would tell you everything you needed. Show you everything, more than you could imagine, and he would allow you into his thoughts. Listen to you, whisper to you, share dreams, make music for you and softly hum it into your ear, so that, in the rhythm of the music, in trailing sentences, you would give your heart to him.

Thus, you both would make something out of nothing, and it would feel as if it had always been this way, as if all the moments in your lives had built up with immeasurable precision for this time together. Your air would be his air, and his air would be yours. A soul of scent particles would surround you both, rising above everyone else, and everyone else would be jealous, wanting to have what you had, sniff your scent, and see the light. Admire you, kneel before you, carry you through the city on days like today, above their heads, like the fortunate ones who had found each other. No one would feel lonely anymore because everyone would know that the other existed, and all that needed to be done was to patiently wait, just like you both had done. Perhaps you would be those others, like an unfathomable riddle, where you let yourself fly above your own head, while your heart is connected to your lover's.

Thus, he strolled on, trying to focus on the things around him, to let go of thoughts about you, to temper his longing for you, to slow down his heartbeat so that he wouldn't be overwhelmed by the opposite of the intense feelings he harbored for you.

Ahead of him, a row of girls with short skirts and hanging T-shirts walked. Like a wall of candy colors in an irregular rhythm, the girls moved ahead, each one happier than the other. They clearly fell from the universe to boost the spirits of the poor Earth-dwellers. To make heads turn. To ignite, taunt, target testosterone. A responsibility they were incredibly unaware of, they continued to chatter carelessly. Unconcerned about the men taken out of their daily worries, colliding with each other with a strange haze in their eyes. The only safe place was two meters behind the wall, and our man praised nature that hip-swaying women did nothing to him.

A regular Thursday evening. Time flowed effortlessly, the street filled with various characters, and he was amidst them. Meanwhile, he thought of you, and because he was a man of passion, the sun was shining. At the end of the street, the excessively sweet wall disappeared before his eyes, and the city behind him seemed to sink away. In front of him was water; he had reached the quay, where a large number of sailboats were moored. Most sails were neatly stowed, rolled up on the boom and tied with flat knots. A few sailboats navigated the open water, trying to find their way into the harbor.

A tall woman stood with her hands on her hips, watching our man as he walked past. He nodded kindly; she looked back suspiciously. Doubt. Maybe he wasn't supposed to be here. But he hadn't seen a sign, nor was there a fence with sharp hooks. He walked to the end of the pier, took off his shoes, and sat on the edge so that his ankles just didn't touch the water below him. Lit a cigarette and sat there until the sun set.

Time. Everything takes time. Nothing is free in the domain of the clock. Time ticks on like a soulless entity that cannot be disturbed. By anything. The hands overlap endlessly. The numbers change into the next and the next. One becomes two, two becomes three, three becomes four. Until six. And then comes zero. Or zero comes after four or after two. It's discouraging. Whether you stand still or run. Whether you sit or stand or lie. Float, fly, or fall. Time. Forever.

And you. Where you are, where you go. Where you live, where you walk. Where you talk and how you laugh. You already have a whole life behind you and more life ahead of you.

You've stumbled over your own illusions once, and you've felt the pain of betrayal as it spread like poison throughout your entire body. Shivering in the cold, you lay in the gutter, unable to stop your body from convulsing, and your heart trying to bore its way to the ground. When you finally stood up and wanted to cry, scream, yell, you had no energy left to catch your own tears. You knew it would never be okay again. That maybe you'd tell a white lie to convince everyone that you had processed the whole incident well. That you had become a richer person. That you had even learned from it. The reality is that you no longer trust anyone, not even yourself, and you've hardened, staring contemptuously at the untouchables, knowing that everyone will be betrayed, and it will never be okay with anyone again. Such is life, and all life is finite.

Only fast love can still warm you. But if that warmth retreats as quickly as it comes, you're left stunned, as if a black hole now occupies the place where your heart once was, dragging you aimlessly through the void forever.

Smile. Forget your head, let yourself be taken in a park and see how dark figures flee from the first rays of sunshine. Stand on a dance floor tripping on your own reflection, walk invisibly through a supermarket, hold onto the walls of the city before it swallows you, guides you through its intestines and squeezes you out as compost.

If you no longer dare to look at anyone, it's your fault. If everyone ignores you, it's your fault. If the world doesn't understand you, it's your fault; you're the one who doesn't understand the world. Meanwhile, men are walking around just thinking about the moment when you both bump into each other. Don't mess it up. Step out of yourself. Forget who you are before your fate is sealed.

It often happens that you bump into someone. That you notice a piece of your heart is still there. That you realize not only your head is in charge. That not all hope is lost. But the thinking wins again. There is that you, the one you can't control, who rushes with his sword, as if every living thing is a danger to be quickly dealt with, as if love were the end of yourself. You see yourself doing it. After the initial opening and the promise of trust, you turn around and burst into laughter. This can't be true. You don't believe in fairy tales anymore. You tell yourself the story of honesty, purity, and authenticity, and then you manipulate it until it clicks for the other. This takes longer for some than for others. Lost time. A matter of lighting. Betrayal, but now with you as the betrayer.

You're sitting at the same table. You keep an eye on each other. You don't laugh at each other's jokes. You try not to understand each other. You circle each other like vultures. Both of you can't grasp the other. You let it be.

You're already with someone else. Someone who once understood you but hasn't for a long time. Someone you lie next to every night without wondering why. Someone who now only irritates you. You call this loving someone. Someone who may have seemed destined for you but, upon closer inspection, is nowhere near. Someone you were once in love with. Someone you spoke sweet words to. Someone you can now best forget. Because your time is up. Time also destroys you. That's why you're here. Running away. Back to something you call home but isn't anymore. Back to a past that has fulfilled its future a hundred times. Back to nothing.

Maybe there's something from the past to save. Like paintings are restored in a museum so you can look at them longer. Like you leave that old shed standing because it doesn't leak that much after all. Like you keep wearing that T-shirt because it once brought you happiness. This happens so often that you don't even realize what you've become. Life has affected you, crept into your bones; it feels like there's no way back. Life has left you damaged, entered your bones; it feels like there's no way back. That canned laughter of yourself, you see it in everyone you meet afterward, and from that moment on, you're quite stuck. If you really understand everything so poorly, maybe you're the most incomprehensible to yourself. Elusive, overripe, almost rotten.

Through the ruse and all the smoke screens, a decision must be made.

But you forget that you shouldn't choose; you should feel.

And if you don't feel it, what reason do you have for all those thoughts? Stop. It's not too late yet, even if you think the end is near. There's still the possibility of redemption. If only you see it. You throw yourself into your work and pretend nothing is wrong. You run through your life, as if you had to catch the train twenty-four hours a day. As if everything were more important than your heart.

No harm, no foul, he who does not dare does not win, and you never know how a cow catches a hare.

Likely a regular Friday morning. The street is empty, people on the boats are sleeping, a plastic bag floats in the water. And while the sun shyly begins its journey through the cautiously blue sky, the train at thirteen past five rolls into the station.

ABOUT THE AUTHOR

GJ Wielinga (1971) grew up amid cows and churches in Northeast Friesland. He has been living and working in Amsterdam since 1992. In addition to being a writer, Wielinga is also an artist and campaigner.

Other novellas in English:

The Digital Version Of My Brain Is One Big Grey Hole (2023)

9 789081 428873